DISCLAIMER

This is a work of fiction. Names, characters, places, events and incidents are either a product of the author's imagination or used in a fictitious manner. The names of a few of the characters have been changed.

Because the dog is the story teller, the rules regarding proper grammar and punctuation are very loosely followed.

Books by Jennifer Rae

Hector's Hope

By
Jennifer Rae

DEDICATION

 To my dear, late husband whose kindness served as my inspiration, his enthusiasm sparked my motivation, and above all, he remains in my heart forever as my very best friend and love of my life.

and

 To the dedicated volunteers of A.R.F. (Animal Rescue Foundation) whose tireless efforts to finding safe and loving homes for forgotten dogs and cats are never-ending.

A.R.F. - Animal Rescue Foundation

THE JOURNEY

INTRODUCTION 1

PART I
HELLO CHEZ SHELTER
1. The Nightmare 6
2. This Can't Be Happening 9
3. First Impressions 13
4. Some Scholarly Advice 18
5. Trifecta of Events 24
6. A New Neighbor 29
7. Make-Overs 33
8. Nigel's Strategy 37
9. Strategic Testing 40

PART II
GOODBYE CHEZ SHELTER
10. Escape to the Unknown 44
11. The Side Trip 49
12. No Guts No Glory 55
13. Transport Tedium 58
14. Destination Hope 63
15. Good News 68
16. Bad News 75
17. The Plan 79
18. Payback 83
19. Lifestyle changes 88

20. New Adventures 96

21. Foster Fun 102

22. Another Escapade 107

23. Wellness Check 114

24. Wicker Chair Caper 120

25. Adoption Mania 124

CONCLUSION 135

Cast of Characters 149

Cast of Characters Continued 151

The Author 153

Acknowledgements 154

In Memoriam 159

INTRODUCTION

While quite the adventurous canine, I filled my life with daily activities that had absolutely no basis in permanence. I really enjoyed the "no strings attached" philosophy because I was actually a free spirit, had no affiliations and no home to call my own.

Before I continue, please allow me to introduce myself. My name is Hector, and I'm a svelte mix of a Chihuahua and a terrier in terms of breeding. My upright ears clearly identify my Chihuahua lineage while the whiskers on my chin undoubtedly label my terrier ancestry. How that combination occurred is well beyond my scope of knowledge. While I am a rather small specimen of masculine strength and determination, I am actually a large, imposing and confident dog in a small, compact body. Some other canines might think I am overcompensating for my size or just plain conceited, but I tend to think of myself as a realist. I know exactly who I am and what I hope to accomplish in my life. Sometimes, I just don't have the skills to achieve my goals, but I can tell you that I am aggressively working towards being successful and reaching the goals that I set for myself.

What were those goals? Well, I once thought that being a carefree vagabond was my calling in life.

However, I can honestly say that, in time, my views about my lifestyle changed. Daily adventures lacked enjoyment, and the unfamiliar need for a forever family periodically crept into my thoughts and often filled my waking moments.

Through the help of canine, feline and human friends, I realized that a better life awaited me, and dreams were mine to have if I only remained hopeful. Discovering that hope enabled me to find my way to a forever home with a loving family.

With any luck, sharing my journey from being stranded and alone on a street corner in the rain to a loving, forever home gives you, the reader, a first hand or first paw look into the various aspects of my situations. Good friends were responsible for changing my life, giving me hope and making my dreams come true. My name is Hector, and this is my story…

PART I
HELLO CHEZ SHELTER

The Nightmare

Ending up in this place was quite the surprise. My last recollection was that of sitting on a street corner in the pouring rain and not knowing where I was. Quite the dilemma if I do say so myself, but fate has a way of stepping into any situation. A considerate man in a passing car saw my shivering, wet body on the pavement and suddenly stopped in front of me. As this handsome man slowly walked towards me, I could tell from his kind eyes that he meant no harm but instead attempted to help. He talked softly to me, wrapped his fleece-lined jacket around my wet body and gently placed me on the back seat of his car. His gentle voice was soothing over the swishing sound of the car's windshield wipers as he slowly drove through the torrential rain. After a while, the driving rain gradually turned to a mild shower as the man pulled into a parking lot of a building called a shelter.

Upon entering the building, the man gently handed me over to one of the workers at the shelter and explained how he found me on the street corner. I wanted to thank him for his kindness in some way, but he left before I had any opportunity to show my gratitude. As the door closed behind him, the warmth of his jacket as well as his scent still surrounded my body and comforted me as I faced a new, frightening challenge. When I looked around the room at all of the wire fencing, I realized that I was alone once again and in a place that held no promise of any future.

I hoped that someday I might see that man with the kind eyes again and thank him properly. While I don't speak his language, I might be able to show him in my own canine way how his actions gave me a semblance of hope for some sort of future…if even for a few moments. That feeling of the warmth of his jacket as well as his scent will forever remain in my memory and will be a source of strength for me as I face challenges in the future.

Uneasiness now filled my mind as I looked at my surroundings. The entire room was dimly lit, had dreary walls and housed rows of kennels on either side of a wide, concrete walkway. Barking dogs were situated in individual kennels creating ear shattering noise and total chaos as I was taken to the area.

I was placed in one of the wire kennels that was larger than a cage and had very high walls made of wire fencing on two sides. A heavy gate of the same fencing material was in the front and had a narrow, rectangular opening at the bottom that certainly wasn't there for any sort of escape. I guessed that opening might be used for serving food and water. At least I hoped there might be food and water. Each kennel had a tall, concrete wall at the back with what looked like a small door of the same, dim color. As I surveyed the entire area, my situation appeared rather grim.

Dogs of all shapes and sizes occupied the numerous kennels. The dogs were either barking, hovering from fear in the cold corners of their enclosures or howling to express their dismay over their situations. Not a single moment of silence broke the cacophony of sounds that resonated through the room.

I wasn't sure what was going to happen to me. One minute I was alone on a street corner in a rainstorm. In the next moment in time, I was in a sturdy, wire kennel surrounded by scary sounds and no apparent way to escape. Even if I had some way of getting out, where would I go? I didn't even know where I was.

Those chilling thoughts brought me to the stark realization that I was here to stay in this horrible place. With that knowledge, I joined in the howling that echoed throughout the building. My biggest fear was that I might not ever stop. My nightmare began…

This Can't Be Happening

Since my last memory was the sound of my constant howling through the fencing that surrounded me, my first thought upon waking was that last night's scary events were all a nasty nightmare, and I had probably fallen asleep from the exhaustion of all the turmoil. I was certain that once my eyes adjusted to the dim lighting of the room, I would think better of my situation.

Then, reality hit me square in the muzzle. As my bleary eyes focused on my surroundings, absolutely nothing had changed. I was still in this horrible, dingy place that was, by all indications, my permanent residence. What happened to me last night wasn't a nightmare at all!

Suddenly, the door at the back of the kennel opened, and I saw light beyond the door. Perhaps it was a way to escape this awful place, or if not an escape route, at least it was an opportunity for patio seating. I was wrong on all counts and faced with the same dingy, concrete floor and strong, wire fencing on all sides. However, the outdoor area had a view of a busy street, and cars sped back and forth without even a glance at the captives behind the fencing. Nevertheless, the view of passing cars provided some break in the monotony of incarceration. Seeing the sky and breathing fresh air somehow gave me hope of perhaps better days ahead.

Those thoughts were short-lived as the barking and howling from numerous kennels overcame the momentary sense of calm that I felt when first going outside. My first instinct was to give in to hysteria which would include my shrieking, rolling around and possibly throwing myself against the sides of the wire fencing that surrounded me. Let's call the kennel what it was…a prison!

Just as I was about to give in to the hysterics of the moment, it dawned on me how much energy that entire process of hysteria demanded. Losing control required a lot of get-up-and-go, and my get-up-and-go left at some point last night when stranded on that street corner in the rain.

That issue of hysteria presented a real dilemma. If I used all of my energy for that process, what reserve strength would I have for the next obstacle? I briefly stopped thinking about flailing around this prison to think about what my next move might be. As I sat on the cold, concrete floor, I was lost in thoughts that swirled around my head like a top spinning out of control. Once I regained my composure, I took a well-deserved breath and unexpectedly gave into the previously proposed hysterics regarding my situation. I howled, barked, whined and added some high-pitched shrieking. For having such a small mouth, I sure made a lot of noise. Emotion overcame me as my noise level increased.

Suddenly, an earsplitting voice coming from the next fenced area interrupted my recital of woes. Sounding as though a megaphone were in use, the rude perpetrator loudly addressed me as Short Stuff and insisted that I cut out the noise because dogs were trying to sleep!

Short Stuff? Who had the audacity to call me by that degrading name? I was a big dog in a small body, and anybody who ever met me recognized that fact. So, I gathered my wits after my hysterics were so blatantly interrupted, and might I add that gathering my wits was no easy task, and proceeded to look around the area to determine who made the rude comments regarding both my stature and emotional outburst.

Looking into the neighboring kennel, I saw a gigantic structure that was either a large black wall or by some freak of nature, another type of canine. Suddenly, the giant image moved and was, indeed, a dog with a head the size of carry-on luggage one might see at the airport. Never in my travels on the street was I ever confronted with such an imposing and scary creature. While the color of his coat was as black as coal, shades of brown markings covered his face as though he were wearing a mask of some demonic creature. His eyes seemed to glow as he glared at me with what I termed the creepiest "stink eye" ever imagined! As I surveyed this tower of strength from head to toe, it quickly registered on me that his paws were the size of hamburger patties with slight markings of brown close to the tips of very long, sharp nails. For the first time since my incarceration in this awful place, I was glad a strong set of wire fencing stood between us. I admitted it. Short Stuff was scared! This frightening situation can't be happening…

3

First Impressions

As this behemoth lowered his massive head and moved toward the fencing that separated us, I felt my mind's image of being a large dog in a small body gradually evaporating. I took a gulp of air, swallowed slowly and took a brave yet risky tactic. I tentatively stepped toward the fencing and introduced myself to the colossal canine who was, after all, my new shelter neighbor.

At first, my introduction was a bit tentative evidenced by my stammering. However, I had nothing to lose. He was, after all, behind a gigantic fence, and I could probably outrun him if by some miracle that huge body could climb the barrier. I had a tightly, muscled body that was closer to the ground, weighed much less and learned some great, defensive moves while living on the streets. But, where would I run? I was surrounded by wire fencing and had no place to hide.

As I talked to him, I stressed my good qualities and left out the ones that pointed to my intense fear. To my surprise, the giant, whose huge mouth was close enough to consider me an appetizer if not for the fencing that protected me, smiled showing the biggest, sharpest teeth I had ever seen. He thought I was quite a brave canine for being a Short Stuff and welcomed me to the neighborhood!

My new neighbor's name was Jake. According to him, he was a breed known as a Rottweiler. He wasn't especially proud of a breed that had the word "Rot" in it, but he felt that his special attributes like shiny coat, good disposition and friendly smile made up for the lack of a classy label.

Having clarified his breed information, Jake shared some experiences from his life. Before ending up in the shelter, he had been chained to a fence in the back yard of his owner's house. He spent all of his time thinking of ways to escape while huddled in a much-too-small hut that was supposed to shield him from the hot sun in summer and icy winds in winter. That form of housing provided nothing in terms of adequate shelter from the elements.

He decided that he was going to escape if it were the last thing he would do. Every day, he tugged harder and harder on the spike-lined collar and chain that restrained him. In spite of the pain and sores that formed on his neck from his struggles, he finally pulled free and was on his way to what he hoped would be a better life.

After weeks of being on the streets, foraging for food and sleeping in doorways, he was caught and brought to this shelter. When he first arrived, he dreamt of running free again but being here for quite some time caused his dream to dwindle. Jake was now resigned to living here, called this place his home and had no future plan to escape. After all, he received food, water, and a reasonable form of housing. Sure, a tall fence surrounded him, but it was better than being chained to one.

Hearing Jake's story saddened me as my body slowly relaxed after the initial stress of facing this neighborly giant. I was never mistreated by anyone before ending up in this place. My only misfortune was perhaps being abandoned or lost. I wasn't sure what happened to me. I only remember being found in the rainstorm by the man with the kind eyes. Both Jake and I were stuck here, but I would never call this place my home.

While it was nice to make a new friend and a big one at that, I was still stuck here with no apparent means of escape. After sharing a few pleasantries, Jake decided to share some thoughts on the subject of escaping incarceration. After all, he had been on his own for a while and knew what evils lurked if not careful.

Since he'd been living on the streets, he encountered numerous situations...some good and some very dangerous. However, he had his size, angry facial appearance and enormous teeth going for him. I, on the other paw, offered nothing but the ability to outrun larger predators and weave my way through alleys and backyards at lightning speed.

According to Jake, if I really intended to escape someday, I needed much more than those maneuvers. I needed to think clearly under the pressure of being caught by some uncouth adversary and to have an additional, scary plan that made me look "crazy" so predators would run from me instead of after me!

Thinking clearly in those times of stress was understandable, but having a plan that made me look "crazy" seemed completely outside the walls of my doghouse! I'd really have to think about the looking "crazy" aspect of his wisdom, but what else was I going to do? Being stuck in this place offered all the thinking time in the world.

Jake was ready to resume his nap. Since I no longer intended to shriek and howl due to my incarceration, his nap would go undisturbed. Now I had some serious thinking to do. After all, the morning was quite productive since I demonstrated my ability to show courage in times of fear, made a new friend and a rather large one at that and proved that first impressions aren't always the correct ones. I had to admit that all of these successful operations were accomplished before breakfast. Was breakfast even served in this place? I really had to make a list of questions for Jake when he woke up from his nap.

In the meantime, I sat on the cold, concrete kennel floor and watched the cars speed by the shelter.

Even though their passing by the outdoor area broke the monotony of my surroundings, I noticed that none of the drivers ever looked at the barking dogs in the kennels. In spite of the loud and continuous noise, we were quite invisible to them. The seriousness of that realization hit me with such force that I gasped for breath, and to some extent, that knowledge diminished my hope of ever being more than just some noise from a kennel. If I weren't seen by them, how would I ever be noticed by anyone, to have hope of a different life or to dream of someday being loved?

While sitting out here in the fresh air, my heart ached. Thoughts of the man with the kind eyes usually gave me hope in times of such sadness, but today nothing seemed to help. Now, watching those cars speed by will never mean as much to me as it did before this moment…

4

Some Scholarly Advice

After conquering my former fears of being incarcerated and thinking about some possible answers that weren't really solutions at all, I found some comfort in the sounds of Jake's breathing. His breath's monotonous cadence lulled me into a state of utter calmness...something I hadn't felt in a long time. I just might be ready to find my way out of this place.

I was totally prepared to take a serious look at my circumstances and draw from my past experiences while traveling as Jake had suggested. After all, I had met quite a few interesting fellow travelers who shared the same hopes, dreams, as well as, the many fears presented by being alone on the streets. A few of their insights might prove relevant given my current situation.

I also met some well-groomed, home-doggies who had traveled at some time during their lives but eventually settled down with a forever family. One dog in particular came to mind when thinking about my time on the streets. A few months ago, I met a rather scholarly Golden Retriever named Kessen.

While casually strolling through a quiet neighborhood, I caught a glimpse of this stately dog posed on his front porch surveying the street...much like a king might oversee his kingdom. He might have been mistaken for a statue if not for the way his copper-colored coat swayed as he turned his head to look at me as I walked along the sidewalk.

Just as I was in front of him, he cordially introduced himself, invited me to join him on his front porch to rest for a while and to share a drink from his water bowl. I readily accepted his invitation and tried to show some reserve in my drinking of his water. However, my throat was so parched from my travels that I just couldn't stop gulping the water from the bowl. Was my behavior ill-mannered after my host was so gracious in offering a cool drink? Absolutely! I'd offer an excuse for my lack of manners, but what would it matter? I already proved myself to be quite uncouth!

Being well-mannered, Kessen never mentioned my lapse in courtesy. Instead, he shared some of his adventures. He had been quite the traveler in his youth and had such an interesting life. He originally came from California as a puppy and following extensive training became a therapy dog who worked with children in neighborhood library programs. To top off those achievements, he was the leader of his canine pack consisting of three other dogs at his forever home. Those credentials were awe-inspiring!

As Kessen talked about his experiences, my mind reeled with excitement. I couldn't imagine how he accomplished so much in his lifetime. How did he manage to do all of those things amidst problems that arose on a daily basis? Kessen recognized my sense of bewilderment over his accomplishments and decided to share his philosophy on life and how living on the streets presented endless problems that needed to be approached in certain ways.

First, I had to "think smart" and view the situation from all angles in terms of survival on the streets. Checking out the areas carefully so as not to enter another dog's territory by mistake was crucial. A dog, especially a smaller version of one like myself, was vulnerable to attacks by larger and stronger dogs defending their territory. Situational awareness was key to survival on the streets.

I must admit that Kessen's information was freaking me out. As far as I was concerned, those tasks were easier said than done. However, I told Kessen that I would attempt to "think smart" while pursuing my vagabond lifestyle.

His other tactic was a method taught to him many years ago by another seasoned Golden Retriever named Linus. The tactic was called the Three Step Plan that almost guaranteed self-preservation. When first approached by an adversary, creating a menacing appearance by curling one's lip and showing as many teeth as possible was essential. If that didn't stop the challenger, a muffled growl was added. Usually, the curled lip, showing teeth and muffled growl worked well in terms of diffusing the situation. However, if the foe continued his aggressive approach, a quick snap of the teeth in close proximity to the challenger's face was the final step in the tactic. That unexpected snap often caused confusion in the challenging canine and successfully turned the adversary away.

After sharing both his "think smart" approach as well as the Three Step Plan, Kessen added his final words of wisdom. As he looked directly into my eyes, I felt as though he were catching a glimpse of my soul. That depth of his seriousness startled me to some extent, and I gulped a bit out of surprise. Kessen's eyes softened when he noticed the alarm in my eyes. While he didn't want to frighten me, he wanted me to realize how important it was to face problems in a calm way. According to Kessen, problems were just solutions waiting to happen.

His considered advice contained some pretty deep thoughts! Following those important words of wisdom, he said goodbye and wished me luck in terms of finding what was important in my life. As I left his front porch, he turned and went back into his house. I never saw him again but would always remember his scholarly advice. I was a lucky dog that day!

As it turned out, I would depend on Kessen's wisdom many times during the weeks that followed our meeting. I called it the Kessen Plan, and those words of wisdom came in handy when faced with an approaching pack of angry-looking dogs, a grocer chasing me with a broom or a feral cat looking at me as if I were on the lunch menu. Amazingly, Kessen's Three Step Plan had a lot more finesse than Jake's acting "crazy" plan, but there were vague similarities in terms of projected outcomes. Go figure!

Surprise of all surprises, I did get pretty good at Kessen's methods and found both safety and solutions to some of my problems while on the streets. Now that I found myself in another difficult predicament, I once again relied on Kessen's words of wisdom.

Just as he advised, I viewed the situation from all angles as I judged the height of the extremely tall fencing that surrounded me. Even though I fancied myself to be quite an athlete, that tall fencing was even too high for me to climb, and going under the fencing wasn't even a possibility since the bottom section of the fencing was only inches from the concrete floor. While thoughts and ideas whirled feverishly around my brain, I finally came to the conclusion that escaping my incarceration was a gigantic problem that currently had no solution. Seemed to be a lot of mental work for a conclusion that was right in front of my eyes from the get-go. Of course, I knew escaping this place was an enormous problem, but at least my need for hysteria was gone.

Suddenly, my thought process was interrupted by the sound of the door opening that led to the inside of the kennel area. Hearing that sound, Jake woke up from his mini-hibernation and loudly announced that breakfast was being served. We each went back into the sheltered, kennel area where an oddly-shaped, metal bowl of some mystery kibble had apparently been slipped through the rectangular opening at the base of the gate and placed on the floor. So, that opening definitely was for the food bowl as I guessed earlier. The food was tasteless, but I was really hungry, so lack of flavor didn't matter. I chewed the bland kibble slowly so it would last a while and watched as Jake inhaled his meal quickly. I decided that going to sleep for a while might give me some clarity regarding my situation when I awakened. With that thought, I curled up in the corner on the concrete floor, imagined the sticky taste of the kibble in my mouth to be a delicious meal of biscuits and gravy and quickly fell asleep...

5

Trifecta of Events

The banging sounds of the opening and closing of the shelter's doors awakened me from my nap with the sticky taste of the mystery kibble still in my mouth. Ugh! Fortunately, there was another oddly-shaped, metal bowl containing water at the front of the enclosure that would hopefully save my taste buds from vanishing completely. While the water didn't cleanse my mouth entirely of the taste of the kibble, the water was enough to quench my thirst after napping.

I kept looking at the shape of that water bowl and wondered how that metal bowl got that strange, warped shape. The way one's mind functions under monotonous conditions was fascinating to me. Any other day, the shape of that bowl wouldn't have mattered at all, but today, I was intrigued by the odd shape of that metal bowl!

After my fascination with the shape of the water bowl dwindled, the noise of the clanging doors brought me back to reality and awakened Jake from the temporary hibernation he called power-napping. Once he shook off his sleepiness and focused on the front doors, he informed me that those loud sounds coming from the doors were signs that certain events were going to take place here in the shelter. According to Jake, knowing what was happening on any given day and knowing how to play the game were keys to successful outcomes. What was he talking about? What kind of a game would we be playing in this dog-forsaken excuse for low-income housing?

Well, as Jake proceeded to explain, there were events that took place at the shelter on a regular basis that he called the Trifecta of Events. People came into the shelter for various reasons, and each event had a special meaning and required certain behavior on the part of the inhabitants of the shelter…namely the dogs. Although I heard there were cats here, I never saw them because they had their very own entrance just as we had ours. We only saw dogs in this part of the building. Unfortunately, Jake was only familiar with the process regarding the dogs but believed the cats had a similar process as well.

A far as the visitors were concerned, someone might be dropping off a dog because they either no longer wanted or could care for the dog because of their situations. Those people never came through the kennel areas and left as soon as they handed the dog over to one of the shelter workers. That event was the saddest because the dog lost a family. What greater sadness was there in the dog's life than to lose the people who loved him or at least pretended to love him for a little while?

The second group of visitors came here to find their forever dog who might fit comfortably into their family. Those were the adoption people, and the dogs in the kennels had to be on their very best behavior for this group. When those people came to adopt, they walked through the middle walkway and looked at each of the dogs in hopes of finding one for their forever home. For this type of visitor, the Rules of Dog Etiquette included no barking, jumping or throwing oneself against the wire enclosure. Visitors walked right by a dog doing those ill-advised behaviors. However, in defense of the dogs, some just couldn't handle the excitement of the situation. Seeing someone look at them gave them hope, and that optimism resulted in very excitable behaviors.

As part of this second type of event, the dogs were supposed to sit upright, show their bright eyes, wag their tails and look lovingly at the people. The smaller dogs usually took the prize with this group. People picked them up and envisioned cuddling them in their arms while sitting on their couches at home. A little dog didn't take up much space, didn't eat much and became a win-win situation for both the family and the dog.

Jake was living proof that no one looked at the big galoot with the huge smile and thought about taking him home. Being such a big dog made him a permanent fixture around the shelter. He tried to make a good first impression when people walked by his kennel but blamed his genetic make-up for no takers. Being so large worked against him. No one seemed to want a dog that could barely fit on their couch but, instead, could be the couch!

The last group of people completing what Jake called the Trifecta of Events were the ones who came from rescue groups all around the country. These kind-hearted and devoted people would come to the shelters and look for dogs in need of adoption. So, best behavior on the part of all dogs was essential in order to impress this group of visitors. In other words, the dogs had to look and behave as though being selected by this particular group of visitors was their only option for a chance at life away from the shelter.

Once the dogs were selected, the people from the rescue groups would transport them to another location and place them with responsible individuals called fosters. The fosters would care for them on a daily basis and take them to adoption events held at a local pet store in hopes of their finding a forever home.

Jake had been through many of these events as he called them and was never chosen. Suddenly, I was touched by the sincerity of his sentiments. While I only knew him for a day, I felt a strong bond with him and decided to stick by him at all costs. If he didn't get to leave the shelter, neither would I. Pledging loyalty was easy in theory when no one was looking to adopt me.

The true test of loyalty would occur when someone was actually interested in me. Honestly, I wasn't sure what I would do if that ever happened, but I hoped I would do the right thing.

Now, it was time for me to think differently about the futility of my incarceration and focus more on something that I find positive about this place. Anything constructive about the surroundings might make the days and nights not seem so terrible. After thinking about it, I decided that the shelter needed a new name. Seeing the wire fencing, the tall gates and cracked, concrete floors left little to the imagination. While challenging my vivid thought process to the fullest, I enthusiastically declared that from this point on, our concrete digs would be known as Chez Shelter!

I was duly impressed with my own creativity since the new name inspired thoughts of fancy rooms, comfortable beds and delicious meals. However, my enthusiasm was short-lived since my announcement was drowned out by the noise from the shelter's residents. The slightest sound set the residents into a frenzy of noise, so no one really listened to my proclamation or even cared about the shelter's name change. The dogs just continued to bark and howl at anything and everything. Jake's newest introduction of snoring in his quest for the Gold Medal in Hibernation was the only new addition to the ongoing racket. This nightmare was definitely not going to end soon. Mark my words...

6

A New Neighbor

Well, I didn't get to prove my loyalty to Jake any time soon. As it turned out, I was getting another new neighbor. A worker in the shelter, who approached my area, had a very nice-looking dog on a make-shift leash. The man stopped in front of the kennel next to mine, opened the huge gate and encouraged the dog to enter the kennel.

I don't mean to sound judgmental nor was I necessarily a connoisseur of dog breeds, but at closer look, this dog looked a bit like an elongated Beagle mixed with another unknown breed having very short legs. His distinct, facial markings were Beagle-like with combinations of tans, browns and blacks, but his body from head to tail looked a bit stretched out much like a Basset Hound. His legs had spotted markings of brown and were a bit close to the ground as well. I had never seen a Beagle who had quite the lengthened body shape and was prone to the effects of gravity by being so close to the ground. Although, judging by this dog's spick-and-span appearance, well-manicured nails, and stylish way that he carried himself, he reminded me more of a visiting dignitary than anything else. He was definitely no junk yard dog!

As my new neighbor surveyed his concrete digs, I came closer to the fencing and introduced myself. Of course, I included all of my good qualities and omitted the ones that related to my negative features. I also included information about Jake who was once again totally dedicated to perfecting his temporary state of hibernation.

Nevertheless, this new addition to Chez Shelter wasn't interested in making new friends. He didn't respond to my courteous introduction other than to indicate that information from the shelter's Welcome Brigade wasn't necessary. He did, however, state that his name was Nigel, claimed to be a descendant of royal lineage within his breed and was only here on a temporary basis.

Well, he seemed quite genteel and perhaps his lineage was accurate even though I had never seen an elongated Beagle as a contender for any awards. However, as far as his temporary situation here at Chez Shelter, I truly believed he was misled. The only thing temporary about this place was the potential of heat on a cold night. Nigel certainly had a lot to learn, but I would help him just as Jake helped me. After all, we captives had to stick together!

After our evening meal, the back door to each kennel opened. Dogs were encouraged to go outside, take in the fresh air and complete any bodily business that was required. Jake woke up long enough to go outside and sit for a while. The headlights from the passing cars and a street light were our only source of brightness, and Jake quickly became bored with the situation. Thinking about some conversation with me, he looked over and noticed the newest guest to Chez Shelter. Since Jake had been asleep when Nigel arrived, he never actually got to meet him. Intrigued by this newcomer, Jake bellowed a greeting to Nigel that not only startled Nigel but echoed for a few minutes in my ear drum. That big dog had a loud voice!

Nigel looked around for the perpetrator of the noise, but all he saw in the dim shadows was a huge image lurking in the darkness. I saw that glint of fear in his eyes that was reminiscent of my feeling when I first encountered Jake's massive size as compared to mine. I didn't want Nigel to be frightened on his very first day here, so I explained that the huge, black structure in the darkness was actually a very nice dog, a Rottweiler, named Jake.

Nigel turned his muzzle to the sky as if he were given information that kennel mates, especially of Jake's size and breed, were less than important in his canine world. If he thought of Jake like that, what must he think of me? After all, I was a small, mixed breed canine, but in terms of stature, my body and paws were all in proportion. That fact had to count for something as compared to his having an elongated physique and short legs!

Just as I made a hasty judgement about Jake when he first bellowed at me, I saw that Nigel was making the same mistake. Given time, I knew our new neighbor would come around to making friends with us. After all, we were in this shelter together. Contrary to what Nigel was thinking, our situations were not temporary at all...

Make-Overs

Boredom set in at a very early stage of our incarceration, and even the slightest variation in the monotony of the day caused chaos among the dogs. If a door opened and closed or a metal food or water bowl dropped hitting the concrete floor, the barking and howling began and continued for quite some time. Jake continued his assault on the opportunities for perfecting his hibernation endeavors. I attempted to evaluate any change in the events of the day hoping for some moments of silence that rarely came.

Weeks went by as people came and went either dropping off a dog, looking for a forever pet as well as those people from organizations looking to select dogs for possible adoptions at their weekly events. In passing through the kennel area, some looked at Jake who was sitting upright, alert and smiling in his own unique way, yet no one seemed interested in selecting him for adoption. Momentary glances my way served as encouragement since I thought that I looked quite awesome, but they almost always focused on Nigel. What did that dog have that Jake and I didn't have?

There had to be some redeeming quality in Nigel that Jake and I weren't able to see. That fact was quite the mystery each time someone walked by us and stopped at Nigel's kennel.

I spoke to Jake about my concerns, but Jake just didn't expend the energy thinking about it. He seemed content to go through the drill of sitting and smiling every time people passed by our area. We needed something to draw attention to us, and I had just the proposal. Make-Overs!

So, in the days that followed, we analyzed each other in terms of appearances, behavior and likeability. Scrutinizing Jake seemed easy to me. He sat at the front of his kennel, smiled that never-ending smile that showed too many teeth which gave him a bit of a scary appearance. He didn't have much of a tail so wagging wasn't his specialty, but he did have this little stub of a tail that wagged up a storm with the precision of a woodpecker enjoying moments pecking at a tree. Jake had it all…except for that smile. Because he had so many teeth and such a wide mouth, his smile was more like a menacing grimace than anything else. That look shouted Guard Dog which was so very far from the truth, but that look was something we could change.

Jake wasn't really pleased that change was in order because, after all, that fact took time away from his ambition of being the first dog to take hibernation to an art form, but he trusted me and accepted my constructive criticisms. Now, he sat on an angle so people could see his tiny tail wagging at top speed, practiced a gentle look and lost that grimacing smile. Not only was I a charismatic friend of small stature, but I was also a magician. He was now transformed into an awesome specimen of a kind and gentle Rottweiler.

I was on Cloud 9 until Jake reminded me that now it was my turn for a make-over. To be honest, until I heard those words, I wasn't quite sure I qualified for a make-over. How does one improve on perfection? As I mentioned that statement, a subtle voice from the neighboring kennel was heard. Nigel had observed my re-make of Jake, was pleased about my suggestions but was now willing and able to offer suggestions for my transformation.

Was he eating some form of mind-altering kibble that allowed him to enter into our discussion? Both Jake and I looked at him in amazement. The audacity to intrude on our efforts toward improving our availability was outrageous. For weeks, he disregarded our attempts at friendly conversations. Now, he expected us to listen to his unsolicited recommendations. His suggestions weren't going to be heard today nor any other day in the near future. I assumed that Jake and I were both adamant about not listening to Nigel, or at least I thought we were.

Jake called me over to the corner of the kennels and mentioned that Nigel had some sort of likeability aspect that made visitors bypass us and look at him. Maybe we were hasty in refusing to listen to Nigel's secrets of adoption success. Jake had a point, but the thought of Nigel giving us suggestions about how to get adopted just made this morning's half-digested kibble ascend a bit in my throat. Jake suggested that we just think about listening to Nigel's offer of assistance for a few days, weigh the pros and cons and then, after careful consideration, make a decision whether or not to accept his offer to help.

Jake's plan was surprisingly on track for a dog who spends most of his days perfecting the art of hibernation. I was impressed with his insights into what we might achieve by listening to Nigel. So, now we had a plan…

Nigel's Strategy

Jake and I spent a few days thinking about Nigel's proposal and decided that listening to his thoughts on advancing availability for adoption might be useful. So, we approached Nigel regarding his offer while we were enjoying the clean air in the outdoor kennel area as well as a moment of unusual silence in this part of Chez Shelter.

I was named the informal go-between for the arrangement largely due to the fact that my kennel area was in between Jake and Nigel's. So far, logic played a part in the procedure, and Jake and I would be receptive to listening to Nigel's advice regarding improvement.

Nigel had been quite a bit friendlier since his offer to assist us and made efforts to share bits and pieces of information regarding his life before coming to Chez Shelter. He was forthcoming in that he really wasn't descended from royalty as he earlier shared. In reality, he was a mixed breed whose owners just didn't want him anymore, so he made up the story about his royal lineage to make up for his feelings of sadness and loss. Now, I really felt sorry for him and wanted to get to know more about him as our time in the shelter dragged on, but listening to his adoption advice had to be the priority before any more sharing of personal information.

Jake and I were a bit excited and now ready for some inspiring suggestions from Nigel for improving our adoption availability. As we walked out into the open-fenced area, Nigel was eagerly waiting for us. He was excited that we were willing to hear his views and positioned himself at the wire fencing that separated his kennel from mine. I was actually thinking that this lesson might be fun. Let's face it…we were starved for entertainment and hearing Nigel address us as if we were students in a classroom sure beat watching cars speed by on the street in front of us.

Nigel's lesson began with his evaluation of our unique behaviors when visitors came to Chez Shelter. He noticed how we sat upright, were well-behaved and looked like respectable prospects for adoption. His conclusion was that our approach was all wrong, and he shared a few of the techniques that worked for him in the past.

In Nigel's opinion, looking eager and willing was a turn off for visitors. They came to Chez Shelter to rescue a dog or dogs, so looking forlorn was one of the keys to success. While a happy dog didn't look like he needed to leave the shelter, a sad dog, on the other paw, needed rescuing!

Nigel demonstrated his technique as he sat with his head slightly down, his eyes looking upward and wistfully at an imaginary visitor. Those steps always drew attention from passers-by and were the reasons visitors walked past us and focused on him. We just didn't look desperate enough for adoption. Granted, no one adopted him as yet, but he was successful in having people stop and look at him.

Those actions seemed way out of the lines of my doghouse since I was always energetic and mostly well-behaved. Looking sad just wasn't something I would feel comfortable doing. Jake thought he might be able to pull off that forlorn look without the smile, and Nigel was definitely getting attention by assuming that sad, take-me-home look. So, we agreed to try Nigel's strategy.

We had a rehearsal of sorts as Nigel looked on to offer any constructive criticisms. I did exactly what Nigel said to do and only had difficulty with my eyes looking upward since doing that just seemed silly. Jake, on the other paw, was extremely successful in duplicating Nigel's instructions. However, I made the mistake of glancing at Jake, and we both burst into howls of laughter. Doing those things to get adopted was either much too awkward or just plain foolish! Nevertheless, we both agreed to try Nigel's strategy the next time visitors came to Chez Shelter. Anything was worth a try at least once! After all, we had nothing to lose and everything to gain...

Strategic Testing

We didn't have to wait long for people to visit the shelter and for us to put Nigel's adoption strategies to the test. A week after Nigel's informative meeting regarding those strategies, visitors arrived and were carefully looking at all of the dogs in Chez Shelter. Strategic testing had begun as Nigel assumed his trance-like, forlorn stance while both Jake and I attempted to duplicate Nigel's bizarre instructions. We decided not to look at each other since that act would lead to laughter in the form of howling and probably barking as well.

Much to our surprise, Nigel's advice actually worked. Two women stopped in front of our kennels and seemed pretty interested in us. Looking like we needed rescuing was apparently working, but our enthusiasm was short-lived. The rubber dog bone of excitement dropped heavily to the concrete floor as one of the women thought Jake was too big and not a dog to be readily adopted. My heart sank as I heard her words. I dreaded this moment since I remembered saying that if Jake weren't chosen, I wouldn't go either.

After all, Short Stuff and Big Jake were two unlikely matched canines who formed a long-term friendship surrounded by wire fencing. We were a great team!

Jake remembered my promise to stay together. He reminded me that he was resigned to staying in Chez Shelter for the rest of his life, and I'd be a fool to jeopardize adoption because of my promise. Leave it to Jake to let me off the proverbial dog bed of guilt.

Bothersome thoughts swirled around my mind as one of the women approached my kennel with a make-shift collar and leash. I looked at Jake and, in that instant, followed Jake's words about surviving danger on the streets. I jumped onto the "crazy train" faster than a tick jumping on an unprotected dog. I barked, howled, snapped and twirled around until I collapsed on the concrete floor from dizziness. Needless to say, the startled look on the woman's face resulted in her quick retreat from my kennel door.

Unfortunately, Nigel was so startled by my craziness that he didn't know if I had some sort of medical issue or just behaved badly. Nevertheless, he got caught up in my antics and had a good time barking, howling and dancing around his enclosure. Apparently, the "crazy train" didn't require a ticket to ride! Jake just shook his head and rolled his eyes from side to side in amazement of not just my foolishness, but Nigel's as well.

After the women left, Jake, Nigel and I decided to assess what had happened. Jake didn't know what to say about the entire situation. On the negative side, we were still here basking in Chez Shelter's lack of luxury while sadly awaiting what had to be some form of mystery kibble for dinner. But, the three of us knew what adoption strategies worked if and when visitors came to Chez Shelter again. On the plus side, Nigel's method of looking forlorn worked for a little while since people seemed genuinely interested. He was disappointed that he wasn't chosen but relieved that I was not suffering from some sort of medical problem that caused my craziness.

Knowing that I was quite a bit more than competent in terms of acting "crazy" gave my fragile ego a bit of a boost. Each day at Chez Shelter, I learned something valuable about myself. Today, I learned that I was still a marketable canine for the right person or group. Nevertheless, in the moment of truth that counts the most in terms of friendship and integrity, as far as I was concerned, promises made were promises kept...

PART II
GOODBYE CHEZ SHELTER

10

Escape to the Unknown

A few days passed, and the three of us never discussed my wild and crazy actions that eliminated any possibility of adoption. Nigel suffered the most because he had the winning strategy for adoption and wasn't chosen because he got caught up in my temporary, "crazy" shenanigans. However, he never mentioned the event at all in the days that followed. Instead, he behaved as though nothing had ever happened and wasn't such a bad neighbor after all!

Of course, I felt guilty about my craziness that caused interested people to move on to other dogs, but it was apparent that both Jake and Nigel had moved past that event and weren't harboring any ill-feelings toward me. I was really relieved and hoped that I wasn't going to resort to acting "crazy" again when an adoption opportunity came our way. I wished there were a way to make Jake look smaller, but nothing short of a miracle made a mountain look like a hill! Just wasn't going to happen.

We didn't have to wait long for the next attempt at the possibility of adoption. On a crisp, fall day, the outdoor kennel area seemed uniquely refreshing as we sat and watched the cars speed by our location. While we were outside, a group of people came to view the dogs in the shelter. The door that separated the indoor area from the outdoor area opened and was usually a sign that something was happening inside. Hoping for an attempt at a culinary delight being left in some form of metal bowl on the concrete floor, we went back into the indoor kennels. We were surprised to see a few people walking through the kennel area.

Nigel immediately sprang into his forlorn, rescue-me look and might have been mistaken for a statue except for intermittent blinking of his eyes. That fact alone was a bit scary! Jake assumed his natural, sitting position and wasn't giving in to Nigel's adoption strategy. He was just a big, gentle dog who wasn't going to pretend to be anything other than what he was. I also chose to reject Nigel's strategy and just sat upright looking handsome as ever. After all, I was a big dog in a small, compact and agile body! Who could ask for anything more?

The people looked like they came from some rescue group and were wearing purple jackets having a dog and cat emblem on the left side of their clothing. Since I couldn't read, the writing under the emblem was gibberish to me, but that fact didn't matter. As they walked through the center walkway carefully looking at all of the dogs, they seemed very interested. This might be our moment!

Dogs were barking and howling at the sight of visitors. Let's face it. We were starved for attention and welcomed any visitors as though they were royalty. Yes, there were some exceptions to the Rules of Dog Etiquette. Barking and howling were occasionally acceptable responses to valued guests. But, Nigel, Jake and I chose to be silent and were now the treasures in the kennels. We just needed to be recognized for our silence.

Being the trio of quiet dogs amidst the howling and barking canines was definitely a sure way to gain attention. As it turned out, the visitors stopped by our three kennels, looked closely at each of us while we portrayed the Trifecta of Treasured Canines…three quiet dogs amidst chaos. We were the pot of high-quality kibble at the end of the rainbow!

As a result, the people of this rescue group were actually interested in all three of us. Our days at Chez Shelter were soon to be over. May the fleas and ticks of the kennels be saddened because the bodies of these three dogs were not going to be providing a time-share for them! Of course, Nigel was totally offended by my flea and tick reference since he considered his body to be a canine temple, but I, on the other paw, didn't care one bit!

We were so very excited about the prospect of leaving Chez Shelter and didn't want to do anything that might make the people change their minds. Nigel and I felt no sadness or regret as we walked toward the front door of the building, but leaving Chez Shelter was a slightly different situation for Jake. He had been in the shelter for quite some time and even considered the shelter his home. As I glanced at Jake, I thought I saw a flicker of sadness on his face.

I fully understood his brief reluctance to leave because the workers in the shelter were kind to him, made sure he had food and water each day and had a warm place to sleep if only on a hard, concrete floor. Needless to say, Jake's look of sadness over leaving was just a fleeting moment. He took one last look at Chez Shelter, picked up his pace and easily caught up with us as we approached the front door of the shelter.

Once outside, we were led to a large van called a transport that held quite a few dog crates of various sizes, and some of the crates already housed barking and howling dogs. We were each gently put in a separate crate and anxiously awaited our departure. The noise in the transport was deafening as the people from the rescue group got into the front seats of the van and prepared to leave.

However, the excitement of leaving the shelter changed for me in the blink of an eye. As the transport started to pull away from the building, I saw the handsome man with the kind eyes, who had saved me on that rainy night, getting out of his car and going towards the front door of the shelter. Seeing him triggered memories of that night...his kindness, the warmth of his fleece-lined jacket as well as his scent that gave me strength to face the challenges posed by being in the shelter. Was he looking for me? Coming to adopt me? Was I missing my chance at a loving home by leaving the shelter? I was frantic over the missed possibilities.

Jake and Nigel saw what was happening, and they started to bark in the hopes of getting the attention of the handsome man with the kind eyes. I joined in the noise but our efforts were useless. The transport's doors were already closed, and the barking went unnoticed as the man had already reached the front door and entered the shelter.

Missing my chance at being seen and possibly adopted by the handsome man was a definite damper on the exciting event of leaving the shelter. However, there was nothing I could do about it. Jake reminded me that we were now about to begin a new chapter in our lives and might look at the change as an adventurous escape to the unknown rather than a dismal ending to life at the shelter.

Jake, in his wisdom, was undeniably correct in terms of his thoughts regarding our futures. If being adopted by the handsome man was meant to be, then perhaps sometime later our paths would cross again. That thought gave me hope for future dreams coming true, and having hope was a much better way to start an adventure…

The Side Trip

The initial thrill of our leaving Chez Shelter was short-lived and remained with us until we reached the end of the long driveway. While looking through the windows of the transport's back door, the view of the shelter gradually diminished and was clearly out of sight once we reached the main road. The earlier excitement over leaving now turned to anticipation and then gradually changed to anxiety once the reality of our situation sunk into our heads. We were in a large van called a transport being driven by unfamiliar people. Add to that fact, we were on a highway going to some unknown place. What were we thinking that being selected for possible adoption might be a very good idea?

By the time we got to the main highway, most of the dogs had already fallen asleep in their crates, and the sounds of various levels of snoring were heard by a few of us who were still pondering our destinies. Perhaps the sleepers weren't apprehensive about the journey to Who-Knows-Where, but I definitely was. While I seriously considered myself as having a big dog's bravery in a bit of a small body, this dog, also nicknamed Short Stuff, was undeniably scared and not afraid to admit it!

Since we were only seeing the highway with its cars, trucks as well as an abundance of trees, the ride so far was uneventful and seemed a bit boring. Nigel announced that he was determined to get his canine beauty sleep while on the road. According to him, his good looks didn't just happen overnight and needed a lot of daily attention. Now he was curled up in the corner of his crate and snoring loudly while his tongue dangled on the side of his muzzle. The sight of him in that condition would be etched in my memory for quite a long time. I was truly sorry I looked at him since his regal image was definitely tainted by this unsightly sleeping pose. We were next door neighbors in the shelter, and yet I never noticed that memorable sight and was now thankful for missing that opportunity.

Jake, on the other paw, was once again making strides toward setting the record for a mini-hibernation while riding in a moving vehicle. That dog could sleep anywhere and under all sorts of conditions that would normally make a dog sleep with one eye open as a precaution. But Jake could sleep where ever he could fit! Gotta love that dog!

My apprehension about this unfamiliar trip to Who-Knows-Where was definitely increasing. Even though both the driver and his passenger talked softly to us, my nerves were a bit frayed. Yet, the soothing cadence of the front seat voices gradually helped soothe my frightened condition, and I felt my tense body relaxing as we sped along the highway.

As the transport began slowing down, I heard the driver tell his passenger that we were going to spend some time at something called a Rest Stop. I didn't understand why we would be taking a side trip to rest since all we did was relax from the time the vehicle left the shelter. However, as a captive in a crate, I had no control over what was happening or where we were going. My role as some sort of contributor to the trip's itinerary was nonexistent.

As the transport pulled off the highway and came to a gradual stop, the sleeping dogs in the crates awakened. The ritualistic barking associated with a moving vehicle coming to a stop began. While the racket was definitely ear-splitting, Jake's dozing was never interrupted. I had to practically bark into his ear to awaken him. As he regained focus from his slumber, I received a very stern look for my efforts. His harsh expression implied that I had ruined his chances for some special award for slumber in a moving vehicle. As humble and caring as Jake was, awards and records for slumber situations meant everything to him.

During his waking moments in the outside area of Chez Shelter, I often joked about his hibernation goals as being self-serving and lofty. His response to my comedy routine regarding his hibernation attempts was to fall asleep while I was joking. Jake was a tough audience, but that fact didn't deter my attempts at humor. Personally, I think he was just pretending to fall asleep and, at the same time, having a good laugh about my comedy routines.

Nevertheless, I admired Jake's ability to let nothing bother him and to look upon each day or new circumstance as an adventure waiting to happen. I wished that I had that same quality since I worried about everything and anything that was different from my daily routine. As Jake regained his focus, he looked around at the area called the Rest Stop and wasn't concerned at all. My first thought was that Jake needed to teach lessons in rolling with the situation. His calm yet cautious approach to dealing with such mind-bending circumstances was undoubtedly skillful. I wasn't jealous of Jake's talents. Instead, I was in awe of his expert approach to situations. He was undeniably the right dog to lead the assault on the large, gravel-filled battlefield. Perhaps my statement regarding the Rest Stop being referred to as a battlefield was a bit too dramatic…even for me!

However, as I looked around the area, the Rest Stop was misnamed in that a lot of action was going on at that location. There were some dogs already in the area who were tentatively mingling with other canines but mostly staying away from each other as they carried out their less than private, disposal business. Nevertheless, from the hazardous condition of the grounds, the area was not meant for rest, new friendships or dawdling. Judging from the treasures left on the gravel, the area was a veritable land mine of bodily business left by canines who were incapable of cleaning up after themselves. Yes, dogs have paws but no flexible digits that enable that sort of clean up. How would we be able to maneuver that area successfully and still maintain a degree of cleanliness?

Our rescuers came to the back of the transport and opened the doors. Jake and I were the first dogs chosen to explore the dangers of the area. I was beside myself with concern over what I considered an infested war zone, shocked at the remnants of canine donations left on the grounds as well as the possibility of stepping on the wrong side of the gravel. Jake told me to relax and wait until he surveyed the area. He had a plan that would help all of us on the transport. Since he was a much bigger dog with significantly larger paws, he was in a more challenging and precarious situation in terms of finding clean space on the gravel. Once he found a safe path, the imprint of his paws would provide a type of map for safe navigation of the grounds.

How does one argue with the logic of that plan? Jake was, indeed, a brave and true friend to consider the welfare of my paws as well as those of the other dogs in the transport. However, he added that his motives were not entirely based on gallantry and friendship. He also took into consideration the location of our crates in terms of being next to each other in the transport. If his plan were successful, all dogs would have access to a safe area as well as clean paws upon their return to the van. That attention to cleanliness would certainly guarantee the quality of the air surrounding all of our paws once inside the vehicle.

Hearing Jake's combination of motives gave me additional fears regarding air quality control on the potentially long trip to Who-Knows-Where. Now, the pressure was not on Jake alone for precision in cartography but on me as well to carefully follow his paw prints made in the gravel. Since Jake and I were the first two dogs to venture onto the grounds of the Rest Stop, we had a responsibility to the other dogs who would follow our leads.

Adhering to Jake's plan was our only option, and spending time at this Rest Stop was doing nothing for my peace of mind. Yes, the side trip to the Rest Stop meant we were stopping, but we were definitely not resting...

No Guts No Glory

Watching Jake traverse the grounds of the Rest Stop was the equivalent of seeing both a battlefield maneuver and the movements of a graceful yet enormous ballet dancer. His measured actions were so precise as he tentatively put one paw down and then quickly withdrew it due to doubts of the area being stable. At that point, Jake turned to another path that might better accommodate his weight and size. He stopped, waited and changed paths before he successfully trusted his instincts to step down with the full weight of his body. Those tentative paw steps took guts on his part with no promise of glory if not successful.

While watching his cautious maneuvers from the sidelines, I was certainly not the only dog in awe of Jake's determination to make this area safe for all of us. Nigel and the other dogs, anxious for their turn in the gravel-filled area, nervously watched and waited for Jake's successful completion of his precarious plan.

Jake's brave actions, as he mapped out the grounds for the rest of us, were a sight to be seen. His movements were an awesome combination of a Five Bone General skillfully fulfilling his leadership role while expertly maneuvering the hazards in the contaminated gravel. Jake was definitely quite a talented Rottweiler, and I was so proud to be his friend.

After surveying the entire area and marking the safe paths, Jake barked his announcement that the area was now secured. Nigel and the other dogs in the transport barked their enthusiastic approval over the successful completion of the mission. I was also voicing my support of Jake's skillful and precise work on the paths. Now, all the dogs had to do was follow his enormous paw prints, do their bodily business and return to the transport with clean paws.

Since the gravel-filled grounds of the Rest Stop had been secured for their safety, the dogs were also barking their praise for Jake's part in keeping their paws clean. He was grateful for their reaction but was also a bit self-conscious about all of the attention. He certainly never got that much recognition while in Chez Shelter and was a bit overwhelmed by the praise.

For just a moment, I thought Jake might use this opportunity to hide from the attention by attempting another one of his mini-hibernations. Surprisingly, he chose to graciously accept the admiration from the other dogs and bask in the glory of a job well done. As Jake walked back to the transport, he held his head high and for the first time, felt great pride in his being a Rottweiler!

Once our rescuers brought us back to our crates, Jake and I both watched as dogs were taken one by one to the secured grounds of the Rest Stop. I could tell that Jake was proud of what he had done today for all of us. He sat upright in his crate as he took in the wonderful sight of the dogs skillfully following the path made for them with his enormous paw prints. Pride was evident in his body language as well as knowing that he, alone, did this for the safety of others as well as for the quality of air in the transport on the way to Who-Knows-Where!

Watching Jake conscious for such a long period of time was perhaps the lengthiest stretch of time I had ever seen him in an awakened state. While stopping at the Rest Stop was initially thought to be such a useless detour in our itinerary, the time spent watching Jake in all of his glory making the area safe for all of us was definitely worth the time spent.

Jake, the Rottweiler, became a legend that day to the dogs on the transport, and I took such great pride in the fact that he was my friend. We were a team, and while we were being taken to some place referred to as Who-Knows-Where, the location didn't matter anymore because we were together. Friendship like that was a gift to be treasured, and I did, indeed, treasure that gift…

13

Transport Tedium

After leaving the Rest Stop and uneventfully cruising on the highway, boredom gradually played havoc with my thoughts. I was much too excited to sleep while my best friend, Jake, was once again vying for the record of sleeping in a moving vehicle, but this time, he was sleeping while sitting upright in the crate. His attempts at winning awards for various positions were unique and endless in terms of variety.

On the other paw, Nigel was fully awake after his beauty sleep and pondering the question as to whether or not the pads of our paws smelled like corn chips. He heard that fun fact said by one of the workers at Chez Shelter but was never able to confirm its truthfulness. Since Nigel never tasted corn chips and wasn't familiar with their scent, he had no basis for comparison or verification of that fact. His hope was to one day eat corn chips, grasp the fundamentals of the scent and test the truthfulness of that theory on the pads of his own paws. He, too, had such lofty goals!

As I listened to Jake's staccato-like snoring and Nigel's constant banter about his theory regarding corn chips, the earlier uneasiness felt about the trip to some unknown place was mounting. My nerves were as frayed as a flea caught in a dog's collar!

The stress level at Chez Shelter was definitely non-existent compared to this trip. At least at the shelter, we were fed, provided with indoor and outdoor accommodations, watched cars when outside to break the endless monotony and, most importantly, we always knew where we were. On this trip, we don't have a clue as to the destination or how long it will take to get there.

That troublesome uncertainty brought to mind Jake's personal opinions regarding my thinking that our situations would be better if we weren't in the shelter. I frequently talked about escaping to a better and happier way of life, but Jake's waking moments were so unpredictable. As soon as he awakened and clearly voiced his opinions, I not only listened but was definitely intrigued by his words of wisdom. When fully awake and focused, Jake was quite a philosopher.

Thoughts of Jake's profound statements such as "the concrete was always cleaner on the other side of the dog run" or "the kibble in your neighbor's food bowl always looked better than yours" filled my mind. If he felt that I wasn't comprehending his wisdom, he resorted to his old standby of "be careful what you wish for!"

I've always been a steadfast dreamer and relied on wishful thinking to get me through troubling times.

However, this trip was shaking my confidence in terms of the good things that come from wishes for changes in one's life. But, if I lost my faith in dreams, hopes and wishes, what would I have left?

I could go on and on with reasons for not being on this field trip to some unknown destination, but then I'd be as annoying as my transport pals. What made my thoughts worse than what my buddies were doing was the fact that I'd only be irritating myself! Apparently, the transport tedium was messing with my state of mind, and my challenge was to find some way to deal with the boredom.

At first, I thought a short nap might help with my anxiety, but I was much too uneasy to sleep. Besides, the roads were not the smoothest of surfaces with their potholes that I called land mines. Being startled by the explosive jarring of unexpected bumps in the pavement would only cause more apprehension for me. I was a worrier in every sense of the word!

Between Jake's snoring and Nigel's issues regarding corn chips, I resorted to thoughts of advice given to me by the wise Golden Retriever named Kessen. I met him during my vagabond days, and he was kind enough to share some well-needed advice about being a small dog and alone on the streets. One important part of Kessen's advice that really hit me in the proverbial dog house was knowing where I was at all times which he referred to as situational awareness. If I modified his advice to fit my situation and studied my surroundings, perhaps I'd find the distraction that would take my mind off my bothersome thoughts. Now, I had a workable plan!

Looking around, the transport wasn't offering much of a solution to my dilemma. The driver and passenger in the front seats talked with each other. Jake was now attempting to win an award for sleeping on his back while crated in a moving vehicle. Nigel was finally drifting off to sleep with his tongue, once again, dangling from the side of his muzzle. Seeing Nigel in that sleep position had the potential for nightmares at the drop of a very small bone. Yikes!

My only options were going to sleep or looking out the transport windows. Since sleep wasn't going to happen, I resorted to a different version of Kessen's situational awareness by watching the surrounding areas through the windows as the transport glided along the busy highway. Seeing the dilapidated barns, occasional farm animals near the fence line and lots of trees helped my situation. Enjoying the passing sights was helpful as I felt the tension gradually leaving my body. My version of Kessen's plan really worked for me!

Now that I felt calmer, I began watching the cars and trucks as they sped by the transport. Some of the big trucks were a bit intimidating as they raced by at full speed, but each passing car was different in terms of passengers. Some cars had only one driver while others were filled with moms and dads sharing thoughts with each other in the front seats and kids playing games in the back seats. I wondered what sort of adventures awaited them at the end of their journeys. I even hoped that one of the passing cars might be driven by the handsome man with the kind eyes who saved me from that terrible, rainy night on the street corner.

Once again, the tendency toward wishful thinking overcame my rational thoughts. Dreamers did that, and I was unquestionably a diehard dreamer. Wishing that I just might see the kind man driving his car while on this highway kept my eyes focused on the road. Watching those passing cars as well as seeing the passengers having a good time, freed my mind of the bothersome thoughts that led to my anxiety. I beat that transport tedium with the advice from a wise dog named Kessen as well as my refusal to give up on having hope and believing in wishful thinking.

I learned a lot on this trip to Who-Knows-Where. As a means of showing bravado, I used to say that I was a big dog in a small body. However, my beliefs in having hope for a better life and faith in the power of wishful thinking were actually my mind's way of making that big dog come to life within me. Those principles gave me courage in the midst of stressful situations and will remain with me forever. Losing those beliefs meant losing the better part of me. As a true dreamer, I guarantee that loss will never happen…

Destination Hope

While the journey from Chez Shelter seemed endless, there was, indeed, an end to the travels. The transport now traveled on city streets as opposed to country highways, and our final destination to Who-Knows-Where seemed close at hand. In response to the slower speed of the van, the canine occupants of the transport began the ritual of enthusiastic barking. Excitement filled the air in anticipation of facing the next chapter of our lives referred to as Destination Hope, and with any luck, no Rest Stop was involved.

After a series of right and left turns on suburban streets, the transport pulled into a concrete driveway and stopped in front of the large garage door of a ranch-style house. Apprehension filled my thoughts as I stared at the huge garage door, but Jake reassured me that anything was better than visiting the Rest Stop. Once again, Jake was the voice of reason and calm reassurance. Nigel, on the other paw, was primping his coat and grooming his paws for his entry into a new environment. According to him, a dog only had one opportunity to make a very good first impression. His intention was to make the best first impression in the history of rescued dogs.

Jake and I both laughed when we heard that statement because Nigel was just being his pretentious self and probably just as apprehensive as the rest of us in the transport. Letting him believe he was making Rescued-Dog History was just a special way of demonstrating our friendship.

As the driver and passenger came to the back door of the transport, the noise level of the barking dogs reached ear-splitting levels. Each of us had our own personal, predetermined notions of what was in store for us, and that apprehension was just increasing as the back doors of the transport opened. The two dogs in the crates behind us were the first to be taken into the house. Then, it was our turn to begin the next chapter in our lives.

The driver spoke to Jake in a reassuring tone as she gently put a collar with a leash attached around his neck, encouraged him to jump from the crate to the driveway and walked him to the house. On his way to the front door, he looked back at me with confidence in his eyes, and I knew everything would be okay. Then, the transport's passenger came out of the house with another woman who would bring us into the house. Nigel was fitted with an appropriate collar and leash, carried from his crate, placed on the driveway and escorted to the front door of the house.

The other woman, whose name I later learned was Ann, gently took me from the crate, wrapped her arms around me and held me so close to her body that I could feel her heart beating. As she carried me into the house, I felt safe and perhaps even loved.

Nigel and I were greeted by the sounds of barking dogs as we entered the house. We were taken through a hallway that led to an area having a fence-like gate separating two areas of the house. Jake was already in the section beyond the gate and seemed comfortable as he explored the surroundings. Nigel and I were taken through the gated area and were greeted by two energetic, mini-sized dogs and one gentle giant of a dog who was even bigger than Jake. I didn't know they came in an extra-large size! Each dog welcomed us in such a kind manner that both Nigel and I felt an immediate sense of relief. As he and I exchanged glances, we knew that our beliefs in hope and the strength of positive thinking brought us to this destination, and the next chapter in our lives held the promise of a good life.

Once past the hallway, there was a kitchen with a table and chairs as well as food and water bowls on the floor. The adjoining room had a fireplace, a large couch, a number of dog beds on the floor and a brown, leather recliner. The mini-dogs were jumping back and forth from the floor to the couch and from the couch onto the recliner as we entered the room. The tan dog was a bit faster than the white one, but they were both quite amusing. Watching them jump around in such an enthusiastic manner was thrilling and was also making the recliner rock in its base. Their antics ended as they jumped from the recliner's seat to its narrow headrest which then served as a perch for them. Seeing them nestled comfortably on the top of the rocking recliner was, in my opinion, a gravity-defying feat. Hopefully, as we get to know each other, they would teach me how to accomplish those thrilling, acrobatic actions. I wondered if furniture privileges were in my future plans while here in this house.

Nigel pranced around the larger room making introductions to the other dogs while Jake mingled with the gentle, giant-sized dog in one corner of the room. At the far end of the room, glass doors opened to a large yard that held the promise of a great exercise area having grass, bushes, flowers and few trees. I imagined myself running laps in a serpentine fashion using the bushes as obstacles. I only hoped I would get a chance for that type of exercise. At this moment in time, my life was really good!

As I looked around the room, I spotted a regal-looking cat having unique facial markings of brown, grey and black. He was, however, dragging his hind legs as he walked. While a stride like that certainly looked uncomfortable, he didn't seem to mind or even care that he was surrounded by numerous, excited dogs of all ages and sizes jumping around the room. I couldn't take my eyes off the ease at which the cat traveled and was thoroughly amazed by his movements. He stopped in front of me, glared at me with eyes that possibly glowed in the dark and commented that staring was an act of rudeness. After that remark, he just glided past me without a second glance and found a comfortable spot in one of the beds located on the floor.

I really wasn't trying to be rude and wanted to apologize because, in my opinion, he was a very courageous cat. Perhaps I'll get the opportunity for apologies later today. For now, I'm just grateful for my good health and the safe journey to this place. However, I must learn to appreciate having the use of my sturdy, four legs even if they are close to the ground…

Good News

Once all of the dogs seemed comfortable around each other, we were allowed into the huge yard for some well-needed exercise. I was thrilled and took full advantage of running around the flowers and through the bushes. Because of this fun-filled activity, the stress of months of confinement at Chez Shelter and in the transport melted away. Those first moments in the yard were so invigorating that I never wanted to stop. However, my legs eventually tired from the strenuous activity, and I found myself resting at the base of one of the trees in the yard. From that vantage point, I was able to watch the other dogs running around and experiencing freedom for the first time after months of confinement.

At first, Nigel was concerned about his paws losing their well-groomed appearance if he decided to run around the yard. Nevertheless, he couldn't resist running at full speed while following my paw prints in the grass. Seeing him let loose in such a free manner was so unlike the refined behavior he often presented as being his true self. Yet, the dog running around on those short legs with his ears flapping in the wind was quite the sight until I saw his tongue dangling off the side of his muzzle almost touching the ground as he ran past me. The earlier serenity that filled my mind was definitely dashed by that fleeting vision. I'll say one thing…Nigel will never be mistaken for royalty as long as he allowed his tongue to flop out of the side of his muzzle at various times during the day. The image of that behavior etched in my mind provided so many opportunities for nightmares in the future.

Jake didn't run around the yard as wildly as both Nigel and I did. Instead, he loped around the yard at a reasonable pace due to his size and commitment to being awake for an extended period of time. Since the environment was new, he didn't want to waste any time for enjoyment of the surroundings by another attempt at hibernation. Was he missing another award opportunity at hibernation in a crowded yard filled with running dogs? Who was this dog, and what did they do with my best friend Jake?

Our new destination seemed to be bringing out new behaviors in each of us. Was that fact the good news or the bad news? Earlier, I was unintentionally rude to the regal-looking cat. Nigel was throwing grooming tips aside by getting his paws wet, and Jake was surely missing the possibility of another award for hibernation amidst chaos. Our world as we knew it was changing for each of us.

When awake, Jake was often the voice of reason, so he would have answers to my concerns regarding our changing behaviors. As he settled comfortably next to me under the tree, rather than discuss my concerns, he took me to task about my comments regarding Nigel's tongue flop as being the potential for nightmares. Jake believed that each of us had a right to our feelings and actions. Nigel was just having fun and being comfortable with himself...tongue flop, short legs, ears flapping and all. His initial concern for a first good impression was just that...a dog having a good time!

Well, my day wasn't entirely turning out on a positive note. Seems my judgement of others was not at all acceptable in my doghouse of friends. So, today wasn't the perfect day I had hoped for in my dreams. Little did I know that Jake's prophesy regarding being aware that the results of fulfilled wishes had definite consequences. How did he get so smart?

Ann, the nice woman who carried me into the house when the transport first arrived, called us back into the house. Perhaps it was good news in the form of declaring meal time, and a delicious bowl of kibble awaited us in the kitchen area. Once again, my score in the good news bracket was still zero. Ann wanted us to rest a bit after running around in the yard with no mention of food being served.

We settled into small groups in the room by the fireplace and made some proper introductions. Jake met with his new, giant friend whose lineage was a mix of Great Pyrenees and St. Bernard. His name was Gus, and he clearly reflected the greatness in size and good disposition of both breeds in his lineage.

Nigel was sauntering around the room like a slick politician running for some public office, making introductions and moving from one dog to another. However, he made sure to mention the possibility of his royal lineage with each and every dog he met. Nigel was such a unique character!

I, on the other paw, was enthusiastically greeted by the mini-dogs when I came in from the yard. They bounced around more than any rubber ball I had ever seen in my life. In between bounces, they described themselves as mixed breeds with Angel's white, coarse hair leaning toward the terrier side and Dino's tan coloring and shape matching that of Chihuahua and poodle origin. Angel thought my keen, upright ears and whiskered chin gave me a most distinguished appearance that outwardly enhanced my Chihuahua and terrier lineage. Dino, looking from another angle, thought that Angel had a vision problem due to her description of me. I gathered from that exchange that there was some rivalry between them, and my outstanding appearance was the cause of their discord. My being a handsome, canine hunk was not my fault.

In order to lessen their rivalry, I encouraged both of them to focus on their antics as being the most wonderful acrobatic display I had ever seen while using a precarious, rocking recliner as a prop. They both responded to this praise and once again began their bouncing around the furniture as though no harsh words were ever exchanged between them.

Their enthusiasm was contagious as I fought the urge to join in their furniture hopping antics and named their acrobatic antics the Rocking Recliner Caper! I was especially interested in the way they balanced themselves on the headrest of the recliner that began rocking as they jumped up and down. I was certain that agility and skill were definitely necessary to successfully complete that endeavor, and I was anxious to learn how they developed the dexterity to accomplish that gravity-defying triumph.

Both Angel and Dino guessed that I was interested in their antics and stopped bouncing long enough to share some of their techniques. I was astonished to learn that strong muscles, high energy and no fear of falling off the back of the headrest were the only requirements. I already knew the floor to couch action, but jumping from the couch to the recliner and vaulting onto the recliner's headrest involved a great deal of skill.

For me, the element of fear of failure entered into the picture. However, I remembered the words of wisdom from the Golden Retriever named Kessen regarding risk-taking. He believed that one only failed if risks weren't taken. If mistakes were made, they were considered lessons for the future. He was one pretty smart dude! Yet, he wasn't the one who was going to jump front legs first onto the headrest of a rocking recliner!

Well, I trusted my instincts as well as the knowledge that my muscular body and paws could climb a steep incline like a mountain goat and would withstand the rigors of that acrobatic feat. Needless to say, I wasn't too anxious to fall off the headrest, but Angel and Dino assured me that I was capable of the maneuver and would bear witness to my attempt. I just had to believe in myself which was easier said than done when looking at the height of that recliner.

Jake, Gus and Nigel gathered around to watch my attempt at what they thought of as a true act of madness. The handsome cat, known as Jasper, was not at all interested in my pursuit of any glory. He slept soundly amidst my attempted acrobatic performance. The other dogs in the room also assembled to watch the show of what might be considered an act of bravery and dexterity or a performance of pure folly. Maybe they were just waiting to see if I might actually fall off the high back of the recliner's headrest. Whatever the outcome, they were all starved for entertainment, so the show must go on!

After taking a deep breath, I launched a running start and easily jumped from the floor to the couch. My audience barked their applause which was a great source of encouragement for me as I faced the next difficult phase of the endeavor. Jumping from the couch to the recliner was a bit of a stretch for my short legs. As I quickly gained momentum, I vaulted from the recliner's seat up to the top of the headrest. I totally misjudged my speed which resulted in loss of solid footing when I finally reached the headrest. My paws just weren't cooperating, and as the recliner rocked, I dropped off the back of the headrest, landed on the carpeted floor and bounced quite a few times before stopping.

Nevertheless, as my canine audience howled their disappointment, I was determined to successfully climb that headrest even if the endeavor took all day. After shaking off the minor aches from the fall, I began my next attempt. As my audience witnessed my second shot at another Rocking Recliner Caper, their dismayed howling turned to enthusiastic barking, and their tails thumped encouragement against the floor.

I began my floor to couch maneuver with the same speed as before, but then rather than gather speed as I approached the recliner, I slowed my jump onto the recliner as well as the vault onto the headrest. This time, my paws gripped the lining of the headrest, and stability was achieved. As I perched high on the headrest of the rocking recliner, I savored the endless barking and howling applause from my audience. I, Hector, took the risk and was rewarded by conquering the Rocking Recliner Caper. Today was definitely a good news day…

16

Bad News

Unfortunately, the well-earned glory of my gravity-defying achievement was short-lived as a few more people came to the house. They gathered in the small hallway with Ann and talked about something called vaccinations. When Gus saw that Jake, Nigel and I were interested in their conversations, he told us that the people coming to the house were called volunteers with the rescue organization. They were going to help with some of the medical procedures as well as the identification process required in preparation for adoption.

Gus, having knowledge of those proceedings, was assigned the task of telling the transport dogs about the health precautions taken after their arrival. He began by saying that each transport dog, who was old enough, received certain preventive measures for health purposes before adoption was even considered. The dogs that came in with medical records might not have to get all forms of prevention depending on what treatments might have been given them in the past. If the dogs did not have any record of medical assistance, they would get a series of special treatments related to prevention of heart worms, fleas, ticks and something for de-worming.

While Gus mentioned dealing with those issues, we had no idea why those matters concerned us. Perhaps he would explain when finished with his information. We would just have to wait for a suitable opportunity to question him.

Silence filled the room as Gus continued and provided us with the next step in our health care. Angel and Dino stopped bouncing around knowing that Gus was sharing important information. Jake, Nigel and I were very impressed with the way Gus commanded the attention of the dogs in the room but were skeptical about the possible treatments that awaited us.

According to Gus, the next step in our journey toward adoption involved getting microchips. Microchips? Were we getting gifts for being rescued from the shelter? What were microchips anyway? Since Gus had no visible hint of a smile on his muzzle, Jake and I guessed we weren't getting any special gifts!

Nigel's mind immediately raced when he heard a word having chips in it and wondered if microchips were somehow related to corn chips. If that were true, he was closer to his corn chip goal and couldn't wait to get one of those microchips. In fact, he insisted on being the first to get one!

Jake and I weren't sure what was going to happen next and looked to Gus for further explanation. While he hated to burst Nigel's Giggle Ball, Gus told Nigel that a microchip was a permanent form of identification about the size of a grain of rice. Each microchip contained a unique, identifying number but had no relationship whatsoever to corn chips. If a lost or stolen pet having a microchip were found and taken to an animal hospital or shelter, scanning the microchip with a special scanner revealed the unique number and eventually led to identifying the owner.

Gus certainly impressed us with his knowledge of the process. However, after sharing all of that important information regarding types of vaccinations and microchips, Gus nonchalantly mentioned that dinner would be served in the main dining room. Apparently, Gus didn't recognize the stunned and frightened looks on our faces due to his information. His references to vaccinations, de-worming and microchips were way outside the lines of our doghouses. At the moment, dinner was the last thing on our minds.

I looked to Jake for some assurance regarding the news, but he was just as bewildered as I was. Nigel was still processing the fact that microchips had nothing to do with corn chips and refused to listen to anything after that disclosure. He was of no help at all!

Was this the bad news part of the day in what was once thought to be a glorious day for all of us on the transport? All signs pointed in that direction if vaccinations and microchipping were involved. Since I believed in the power of wishful thinking, I hoped that what Gus just told us was a figment of my imagination. I probably dozed off from the exertion of the recliner caper and was simply dreaming. Maybe bouncing off the floor following the first rocking recliner attempt left some temporary brain disturbance. Nevertheless, if my dreams and possible brain impairment issues weren't involved, and Gus told the truth, I had to have a definite, evasive plan to avoid those precautionary measures for myself. What I personally knew with the utmost certainty was the undeniable fact that if and when it was my turn for those health procedures, I wouldn't go willingly. While I cared for Ann and the safety I felt when near her, she would unquestionably have to catch me first…

The Plan

After attempting to digest the scary, health care information, Jake, Nigel and I discussed what just happened. Apparently, I wasn't dreaming about the information and thankfully suffered no superficial brain disturbances. I quickly devised a plan that had the potential for saving me from vaccinations and getting a dreaded microchip. Was I being selfish by not sharing my plan with Jake and Nigel? I certainly was, but Jake had much too much integrity to keep my secret from the others, and Nigel would give it up at the wag of a tail if promised a bag of corn chips. My plan had to remain a secret and only worked with a dog my size. Being a Short Stuff definitely gave me an advantage in terms of this caper.

While carefully recounting the information, the three of us centered on the de-worming aspect and wondered why it was such an important part of the procedures. We would certainly know if we had worms crawling around in our intestinal tract. If by some remote chance we did have worms, we undoubtedly got them at that Rest Stop. Wouldn't we have to eat worms in order to have them? We looked to Jake for answers to our questions, but he was just as puzzled as we were. Nevertheless, I guarantee that nothing, not even wiggling worms, touched our muzzles while at that Rest Stop. We just followed Jake's path in the gravel, did our business and raced back to the transport as quickly as possible. Besides, the only things that I saw moving at the Rest Stop were flies!

At first, Nigel was insulted that one might even think his body held something as disgusting as worms. Yet, after careful consideration, he chimed in that in some areas of the country, worms were an edible delicacy when found on driveways after a rain shower. Leave it to Nigel to come up with that bit of culinary trivia. He went on to insist that he had a sophisticated palate, never tasted worms and wasn't even interested in eating them. Being a picky eater, Nigel had a strict rule about not eating anything that moved. Since worms wiggled, they had no chance of ever becoming part of Nigel's brunch menu. His goal still involved eating corn chips and deciding if the pads of his paws smelled like them. However, that corn chip challenge made his claim of having a sophisticated palate a bit doubtful!

Jake reminded us that we had to keep our eyes on the Blue-Ribbon Prize of eventual adoption in a forever home. If getting vaccinations and a microchip would help us get adopted by a forever family, then we had to do our part and cooperate with these nice volunteers. Once again, Jake sounded sensible since we all had hopes for finding a loving, forever home. Why must Jake always be the sole voice of reason? Just when I was all set to object strenuously when it was my turn for vaccinations, Jake set us straight using common sense and reminders of our goals. He was quite the powerful motivator, and even Nigel was impressed.

After carefully considering Jake's remarks about the upcoming health-related events, I had to rethink my earlier reference to being uncooperative when it was my turn for the health care treatments. Yet, I wasn't totally convinced that cooperating was right for me. While I valued Jake's opinion regarding cooperation leading to our goals, I had to be true to myself and study all angles of the situation. After further deliberation, my belief in the power of wishful thinking as well as the importance of situational awareness, I'm sticking with my original statement regarding the health treatments. Short Stuff had a workable plan. When my turn came for Ann to give me the vaccinations and microchip, she'd definitely have to catch me!

One by one, the transport dogs were led by volunteers into the other room for their treatments. Jake and Nigel were already getting their vaccinations and microchips as indicated by the whimpers and howls coming from the other room. I attributed those sounds to Nigel since he considered his body a temple that was being desecrated for health purposes. Jake came out of the room first and gave me a somber but encouraging look. Maybe the treatments weren't as bad as I thought. Nigel followed Jake out of the room, gave me a serious look and made me promise that under no circumstances should I look at the size of the needles. I really didn't need to hear that bit of advice.

When it was my turn for vaccinations, I ran around the room, slid under the kitchen table, hid behind the recliner and made a series of unsuccessful evasive moves. In spite of my extensive efforts to avoid capture, Ann finally caught me. However, she had a lot of help from a silent adversary looking for payback, and I, Hector, the acrobatic hero of the day never saw it coming…

18

Payback

To fully understand the failure of my plan to avoid capture from Ann and the health measures, one needed to look back to a particular incident that occurred earlier in the day. While the event wasn't important to me at the time, I'll explain how I paid the price for it later in the day.

Prior to running around the yard and during our informal introductions, I saw the stately cat with the distinctive gait coming my way. Because I had never seen a cat moving in that manner, I unknowingly was staring at him. After glaring at me with glowing eyes that made "stink eye" look like kitty play, the cat took me to task for what he considered rude behavior. I was so taken aback by the glare of those penetrating green eyes that I never intended to be rude nor did I take the opportunity to apologize. The cat just glided away and settled on one of the dog beds in the area.

I thought that was the end of the situation and promised myself that I would apologize at some time during the day. Well, that apology never happened as I was caught up in the performance and success of the

Rocking Recliner Caper. I allowed pride to get in the way of making amends for my unintended rudeness. I never gave the incident another thought, but I wasn't left off the proverbial pinch collar for my actions either. My unintended act of rudeness left without an apology came back to haunt me in a very strange way. Some might call it karma as I was held accountable in a bizarre manner for my lack of apology to the cat. I, on the other paw, called it blatant payback!

Just after Jake and Nigel had their medical treatments, I heard Ann calling my name, and the call to battle was heard loud and clear. I immediately sprang into action and searched for the areas I had deemed safe earlier in the afternoon. The first place was located in the kitchen behind the large bag of kibble. However, that bag wasn't there anymore and must have been moved after I declared that space as my safety zone.

My next choice was to hide behind a large dog bed that flanked the fireplace. Jake had been lounging in it earlier. All I had to do was position myself behind him when he went to sleep on that bed. The location was perfect, but when I looked across the room from the kitchen, I saw an empty bed. Why in the world of canine capers did Jake decide to stay awake on this particular day when his repeated attempts at various hibernation awards meant more to me than to him?

Now, I was getting desperate as Ann was looking through every room in the house for me. She inspected everything from looking behind throw pillows on the couch to checking under overturned dog beds in search of me. When she went to the other side of the house, I had to rely on my last possible hiding place. There was a narrow space between the back of the couch and the wall that was my best bet for avoidance of needles and a microchip. Being a small dog, I fit comfortably behind the couch, and even if Ann found me in that narrow space, she wouldn't be able to reach me before I ran out the other end of the couch.

It was the perfect hiding place until it wasn't. Apparently, the earlier event that occurred dealing with my unintended rudeness finally caught up with me. Payback time was waiting for me in the form of that large, stately cat. He was sitting at the other end of the tunnel-like area behind the couch and blocking my escape from his end. I immediately recognized those scary green eyes as belonging to the cat named Jasper that I had offended earlier. The frightening grin on his face widened. While showing a hint of sharpened teeth, his whiskers seemed to move in slow motion yet not giving any hint of what was to come. He mentioned the earlier hurtful event and how revenge was oh so sweet. In silent, cat-like motion, Jasper began gliding toward me using only his front legs. He actually looked freakishly amused while showing a bit more of his sharpened teeth while his knife-like nails gripped the carpet tearing just a bit of fabric with each step. I was absolutely terrified of what was going to happen to me. I never meant to be rude to Jasper and really intended to apologize earlier but forgot about the incident. Apparently, this was just not the right time for an apology either!

Hearing Ann's voice behind me was like that of an angel saving me from this terrifying cat. Jasper was scarier than any needles or microchip could ever be. I slowly backed out from the narrow space behind the couch while keeping my eyes glued on Jasper's movements. Ann was waiting for me, picked me up and didn't look too pleased. At least, I was safe once again in her arms.

As Jasper came out from behind the couch, he snickered about my fearful reaction to him. Gus told me that Jasper was just messing with me and was, by far, the kindest cat they ever had in Ann's house. Jake tried not to laugh at my fearful reactions but couldn't resist. Nigel, rolling around on his back while laughing, risked messing up his well-groomed coat. Great Friends!

I deserved every bit of the laughter heaped upon me by my canine friends following the Jasper the Cat incident. I was so taken with my rocking recliner victory that I didn't take the time to think of others and their feelings. I made a promise to myself that I would think of others and their feelings in the future.

Ann took me for my medical treatments, gave me my vaccinations as well as my microchip. Getting them from her, someone I fully trusted, made all the difference in the world. As Nigel suggested, I didn't look at the size of the needles when vaccinated. He was a true friend for giving me that instruction. When all procedures were completed, Ann told me how brave I was. It only took a scare from Jasper to get me there.

As I was heading toward the room where the other dogs were sleeping, I saw Jasper waiting for me at the doorway. Once again, the image of those sharp teeth and saber-like claws reminded me of the fear I felt earlier. Rather than take me to task again regarding my so-called rudeness, Jasper wanted me to know that there were no hard feelings between us. He was glad I was now protected and healthy enough for adoption. I must admit that I didn't expect that response from Jasper but was certainly glad he offered it.

Looking around at the dogs sleeping in various beds throughout the room, I had to admit how very lucky I was. I wasn't even envious that Jake found a new, giant-sized friend in Gus. Nigel still complained about the slight possibility of having worms as well as his endless goal of finding corn chips. Dino and Angel continued to bounce enthusiastically on the furniture, and Jasper even smiled at me once in a while. My life was good evidenced by my having good friends and a safe haven run by a caring woman. As a dreamer, I still had my hopes and wishful thinking for a forever home. What started out as a bad news day really turned into a very special, good news day…

87

Lifestyle Changes

Getting those health procedures really took a lot out of us in terms of get-up-and-go. Following dinner and a trip to the yard for business purposes, we couldn't wait to get some well-deserved sleep. Jake, Nigel and I positioned ourselves on various dog beds located in the room with the fireplace. Needless to say, we were exhausted from the stress as well as the changes that were taking place in our lives. These new challenges that took over our lives were daunting to say the least.

Of course, Jake decided not to worry about things he couldn't control and would evaluate events as they occurred. I really envied his philosophy. Unlike Jake, I made checklists of every possible change that might happen in the days to come. According to Jake, my troublesome thinking would only end up with an increase in stress and restless sleep. Jake was right, but I believed that worrisome thinking was beyond my control. As for thinking of myself as a tough dog in a small body, I had very little confidence in my ability to control my thoughts. I guessed that I wasn't as tough as I thought.

Jake decided to get some sleep while on his back with his paws in the air. Apparently, he was trying for a new variety of hibernation award. From the position of my bed next to him, the air movement resulting from his huge paws waving back and forth as he slept and snored provided quite the change in air flow and was just what was needed on such a warm night. While Jake didn't know it, he earned a special award for climate control!

My positioning for a good night's sleep wasn't well thought out as my bed was facing Nigel's bed. Staring at him snuggled in his bed was comforting to me until he rolled over. The movement of Nigel's body caused his head to hang over the side of the bed. That motion caused his unappealing tongue to hang out of the side of his muzzle. Because of the position of Nigel's head, his flopping tongue waved back and forth with each snorted breath as though a metronome were guiding his tongue's movements. Those dreadful sights and sounds were the basis for all nightmares that made restful sleep impossible.

Gus witnessed my dilemma as I tossed and turned in my bed trying to escape the vision of Nigel's sleep show. Being a kind-hearted dog, he believed we were guests in his house, and his obligation was to see to our comfort. That being said, he immediately knew how to solve the dilemma of my attempted, restful sleep with the least amount of disruption. All Gus had to do was position himself between the two dog beds. As he dropped to the floor in a position suitable for sleeping, his huge body blocked the view of Nigel's bedside show, and the problem was solved. Now, I could sleep without the fear of a nightmare dealing with Nigel's sleep position and instead have good dreams about the kindness shown to me by so many dogs in this wonderful house.

I woke up early and felt refreshed after a good night's sleep. Since Gus was still sleeping in front of my bed, I had to quietly maneuver around his body so as not to wake him. He was so kind to position himself in such a way that Nigel's sleep show was out of my sight. His heart was just as big as his body, and I wondered if all large dogs were as kind as Gus. Jake was just as caring in so many ways. I decided that large dogs having big hearts shared the same greatness of spirit and kindness towards others.

The dogs were slowly waking up and anxiously awaiting a romp in the yard. When Ann came into the room, I thought she might still be miffed at me for my evasive antics yesterday, but she greeted each of us with a wink and a grin. Today was going to be a good day…I could feel it in my Short Stuff bones.

After breakfast, Jake, Nigel and I learned that today was a very special day. We were going to meet our fosters for the first time. I remembered Jake telling me that fosters were volunteers who cared for the dogs each day and brought them to something called events that might lead to adoptions. Those occasions sounded like fun until Gus mentioned that each of us would have that same opportunity to meet our foster today. Weren't we going to stay together at Ann's house? I was stunned to hear that each one of us would go to a different foster and live with them until adopted.

While Jake and I were a team and vowed to stick together, Nigel wanted to stay with us as well. This day was not turning out the way I had imagined. Yet, nothing would change what was going to happen to us. Maybe Gus was wrong, and the other transport dogs were the ones leaving today. Jake pointed out that Gus never gave us false information or misled us in any way. We were doomed and faced with lifestyle changes that involved losing the support of each other.

Waiting for the inevitable doom-and-gloom dog bone to drop on our lives, I spent time during the day as the only guest to my very own pity party. I just couldn't shake the impending feelings of loss that would occur when the volunteers came to the house. Staring out the tall, glass doors leading to the wonderful yard was the perfect setting for feeling sorry for myself. What seemed worse was doubting my faith in hope and wishful thinking. I thought Ann's house was the perfect setting for having hopes and dreams. Maybe I was foolish to think of myself as a dreamer since none of my dreams were coming true.

Jake was convinced that he would stay with his foster forever since no one really wanted to adopt a large dog. He learned that fact following quite a long stay at Chez Shelter. Nigel, being typically Nigel, was convinced that once the fosters took a look at him, there would be a bidding war for him. After all, he was of royal lineage…in his dreams!

Jake and Gus played in the yard a bit while Dino and Angel kept me busy with their lively antics. In spite of my feeling sorry for myself, those two dogs really made me laugh, and I thoroughly enjoyed their zest for life.

The sound of the doorbell ringing sent a chill down my spine. Jake, Nigel and I rushed to the gate that separated the rooms in anticipation of the arrival of the fosters. Jake was determined not to grin since seeing his teeth gave the impression of meanness. Nigel backed up from us and tilted his head to the left since he considered that side to be his most photogenic. He assumed a serious, regal stance so the fosters had the opportunity to acknowledge the presence of royalty. Thankfully for the sake of all of us, Nigel kept his flopping tongue in his mouth! I, on the other paw, remained aloof and would not be easily won over by strangers. In my world, respect was earned. Jake just rolled his eyes and laughed at my silliness.

The fosters were very excited about meeting the dogs. Jake's foster was a tall, good-looking man who had fostered large dogs before and was anxious to form a bond with Jake. He took him into the other room, sat on the couch surrounded by Dino and Angel bouncing around and talked softly to Jake. I could tell that Jake and his foster had the beginnings of a good friendship. While I was somewhat sad to see Jake's loyalty shifting to this new person, his happiness meant more than the loss I felt.

Nigel was basking in the comfort of his foster's cradling and whispering sweet nothings into those large, flappy ears of his. I could tell from Nigel's body language that he believed his foster acknowledged his royal lineage. Perhaps I imagined my self-recognition of Nigel's regal heritage since he so desperately needed it for himself. Surprisingly, I was happy for him to have found someone who would treat him nicely if only while fostering him. He deserved all of the kindness someone could give him, and I have no doubts that his new foster would scrutinize anyone interested in adopting him. After all, Nigel was a self-proclaimed royal!

I was truly happy for each of them, but unhappy for myself because I was the only dog left without a foster. The other two transport dogs met their fosters and were spending time in the other room getting acquainted. At first, I thought I might be staying here at Ann's house. Gus, who knew everything that went on in this house, told me that all the transport dogs were going to fosters.

I sat alone by the gate and faced the distinct possibility of another rejection. Sure, my situation was far from being abandoned on a street corner in a rain storm or being overlooked by visitors in a shelter looking for a forever dog. I just didn't understand what was happening. After all, I was a nice dog, but no one seemed to recognize that quality. I wasn't dignified like my best friend Jake nor was I obsessed with cleanliness or corn chips like Nigel. I was just a small, compact mix of Chihuahua and terrier with a kind heart and a nickname of Short Stuff. Not knowing what was going to happen to me caused me to doubt my having dreams, hopes and even wishful thinking.

I went into the other room and saw Jake, Nigel and the other transport dogs now running and playing in the yard with their fosters. As I sat by the glass door leading to the yard and watched their interactions, the dark cloud that hovered over my thoughts got even darker. Feeling so sorry for myself as well as the loss of self-worth made me a real sad-sack, but I just couldn't help myself. I suddenly wondered what happened to that confident dog who successfully completed the Rocking Recliner Caper? Today's feelings of self-pity just don't reflect the real me. I had to find a way to get that dog who vaulted to the headrest of a rocking recliner back in the game.

Just as my wallowing in self-pity reached monumental proportions, the doorbell rang. I didn't even bother to go to the gate to see who was there since

I was so taken up with my rejection drama. Suddenly, I heard my name being called by a woman standing by the gate with Ann. Evidently, she was my foster and very eager to meet me. Nevertheless, the feeling wasn't quite mutual because of my sadness over leaving Ann's house, losing my friends to another journey in their lives and feeling rejected because I wasn't chosen at the same time as the other dogs. If I don't shake off this aura of self-pity, my foster might turn around and walk out of my life before she gets to know me. No one wants to meet a sad-sack let alone take one home. Was I deliberately sabotaging my chances for a forever home by behaving in this manner? If only I had a day without a dilemma!

Jake and the other dogs came rushing in from the yard with their fosters. When he noticed my doom-and-gloom expression and saw my foster waiting in the doorway, he encouraged me to snap out of it and get with the adoption program. He believed challenges were part of our daily lives and held the promise of extraordinary adventures and happiness. If I really wanted my dreams to come true, I would have to bite the biscuit, leave the past behind, put on my best smile and meet my foster with hope for the future.

Hearing Jake's encouraging words made me realize that I was the only one holding myself back from my dreams. That being said, I put on my best smile, assumed my confident swagger and rushed to meet my foster...

20

New Adventures

Now, all of the transport dogs and their fosters went into the yard for a last bit of fun together. This time, I was out there with Jake, Nigel and the others. While our fosters watched as we ran around together for the last time, our enthusiasm was evident. Nigel's running around the bushes and flowers on those little legs with his ears flapping and tongue hanging out the side of his multi-colored muzzle seemed endearing to Jake. Nevertheless, I really liked Nigel a lot, but seeing those images were far from charming in my eyes. To me, that trifecta of sights always was and always will be the makings of a very intense nightmare!

When our time in the yard ended, our fosters, equipped with collars, leashes, food, treats and toys, called us into the house for our last goodbyes to Ann and her dogs. Gus, the gentle giant, nodded to us and wished us well on our journey. Dino and Angel gave us their version of a sendoff by making one last vault onto the headrest of the rocking recliner. For the last time, Jake, Nigel and I laughed at their fun-filled antics but would remember the image of those little dogs and their defiance of gravity. Every time I see a bouncing rubber ball, I will think fondly of them and their friendship. Jake, Nigel and I wished each other well as we began this new chapter in our lives, but I somehow knew we would see each other again.

As our fosters took us to their respective cars, I thought about the last few days and how each of our lives had changed. We went from a lonely shelter to a safe house filled with new friends. Now, we were moving on to another new and exciting journey.

When I was placed in a crate in the back of my foster's car, I thought about re-living the transport experience from the back of yet another type of vehicle. My only hope was that the ride to the foster's house did not include a side trip to a Rest Stop. If Jake were here, he'd tell me to just roll with the situation. When Jake was fully awake, which wasn't too often, his wisdom was flawless. I intended to follow his sound advice and find something positive about this new adventure.

After leaving Ann's house and enjoying the ride, I glanced over to a passing car and saw Jake in the front seat. He was sound asleep in the passenger seat of his foster's car with his head and huge, front paws balanced on the dashboard. Goodness gracious...that dog never missed an opportunity for a hibernation attempt. Only a large dog had the capability to keep that pose while sleeping. There just had to be an award for that attempt because I never saw anything like it and probably won't ever see it again. Jake's got game!

While still laughing about Jake's hibernation attempt, I felt the car slowing down as it entered the driveway of another ranch-style house. My new foster announced that we were finally home. However, that reference to a place called home seemed foreign to me. I don't remember ever having a real home before, and my understanding was that this placement might be temporary if someone wanted to adopt me. Well, I refuse to ruin this day by thinking about something that might never happen. Apparently, Jake's wisdom was definitely rubbing off on me, and my swagger was returning. Short Stuff was back!

My foster put a collar connected to a leather leash on me, took me out of the crate and placed me on the driveway. As we approached the front door, I was startled to see two concrete statues of large dogs in sitting positions…one on either side of her front door. Seeing those concrete dogs was a sign that my foster really liked dogs. Now, I was ready to enjoy myself.

The entry way of the house opened to a large room that had numerous opportunities for jumping and bouncing around. I wasn't aware of having any furniture privileges, but the prospect of jumping from place to place was encouraging. As I glanced around the room, my heart skipped a beat. In the far corner of the room, I saw a leather recliner just like the one in

Ann's house. Now, I was determined to behave appropriately in order to get furniture privileges.

As we passed the recliner, I lingered just a bit to determine the potential of duplicating the Rocking Recliner Caper completed at Ann's house. All I needed to do was jump from the floor to the seat and vault to the headrest. That entire maneuver seemed relatively easy. However, I still had to view the rest of the house and see what other potential challenges awaited my gravity-defying expertise. This great foster placement was becoming a dream come true. What would Jake and Nigel think about all of this good fortune?

After seeing this room, we went to another room my foster called the sunroom. There, in the corner of the sunlit room, was a large, wicker chair that had the possibility of an additional challenge. This chair faced a window that opened to a huge, fenced yard. The top of the chair was narrower than the recliner's headrest and posed a much higher level of difficulty. My mind reeled with opportunities as I studied the size and shape of the headrest. Leaping to the top of that chair held the likelihood of a Gold Medal in Chair Vaulting. I already sniffed the scent of success in the air.

From the sunroom, my foster took me outside into an area that she called the dog run. The area was surrounded by a white picket fence and had ground cover reminiscent of that material found at the Rest Stop. However, this area was cleaner than any space I had ever seen and not a land mine in sight. Relief flooded my body as I assessed the surrounding area. There was no need for Jake's huge paw prints to make a safe path in this dog run!

At one corner of the dog run, a gate opened to a huge yard filled with trees, bushes and varieties of colorful flowers. A fence surrounded the property, but the space between the fence rails was large enough for me to escape if necessary. As if she read my mind, my foster looked at me and shared that I had to be kept on a leash at all times while she was responsible for me. The thought occurred to me that perhaps she could read minds. If that were true, I had better scrutinize my thoughts. I wonder what Jake and Nigel would think of that mysterious power? Jake would probably encourage me to be extremely cautious regarding my unfiltered, thinking sprees. Nigel, on the other paw, would be impressed and consider her a talented mind reader. He'd probably ask her to share some of her tricks of the trade!

Since there were so many opportunities for new adventures right here in this house and in the yard, why would I even think about escaping? I'm determined to be the best rescue dog my foster ever had, and one who will hopefully gain furniture privileges in the near future. Having good behavior as a means of achieving a goal of furniture hopping wasn't exactly well-intentioned, but thoughts of successfully competing on that recliner as well as the more challenging chair in the sunroom repeatedly bounced around my cluttered mind. Jake always said that having goals led to challenges that were part of an adventurous life. Would he approve of my actions? Probably not! However, in his absence, I will adapt his guidance to fit my goal of being the best rescue dog ever and, as a final result, gain furniture jumping privileges. Let's face it...it's a win-win situation for both the foster and for me! I love it when a plan comes together...

21

Foster Fun

After a long walk in the yard, my foster took me through every room in her house. She wanted me to be acquainted with the layout so I wouldn't be tempted out of curiosity to enter a room with a semi-closed door. I thought she might have guessed that I was inquisitive by nature. This particular foster was one smart woman.

After the tour, we went into the kitchen together. In one corner of the room, I saw a food and water bowl station that was a bit elevated for my comfort. Because of the height of the station, I wouldn't have to bend to the floor to eat my meals. To say the least, I was impressed with my foster's preparation for my arrival. However, the water bowl was the only one in place, and the opening for the food bowl was empty. Perhaps I was only getting water for dinner tonight which didn't seem fair at all. After all, I had been through a lot of changes today and always had a hearty appetite.

As I looked to my foster for some explanation, I saw that she had my food bowl in her hands. I was exhilarated by my good fortune. Not only would I eat in comfort since I didn't have to bend to the floor for my food, but the bowl would be right in front of me for easy access to whatever delicacy she had for me. As I jumped and twirled over my good fortune, my foster just stood in front of the food station with the bowl in her hands. What was she waiting for? I was only able to twist and turn for a limited time since my legs were so short, and my energy level was low due to not eating since breakfast. Tired from the excited antics, I sat on the floor and just stared at the empty space where the food bowl was supposed to be located. Seeing my sitting position, my foster immediately attempted to put the food bowl into the vacant spot on the feeding station. Overcome with excitement over the impending meal, I jumped up from the sitting position and twirled again. My foster immediately stood up with the food bowl still in her hands. Was she teasing me with the food? Did the Foster Book of Canine Care have The Art of Teasing as one of the chapters?

I assumed a sitting position and took a moment to figure out what was happening. Once again, my foster attempted to put the food bowl into the station. This time, I fooled her and maintained my sitting position because I was actually much too tired to twirl around. Suddenly, she put the food bowl in its place. I wasn't quick to move toward the bowl in case she took it away again, but then she told me it was okay to eat.

All evidence pointed to my foster as being a gamer and a tease! This foster placement was going to be fun since we were matching wits. However, in the game of wits, I was top pooch!

The food was actually the same food that I had at Anne's house, but my foster added small pieces of poached chicken and some green beans. I savored every morsel of that meal and considered it the best meal I had eaten in ages. Now, I was looking forward to any games she might play when breakfast came. Game on! It was foster fun time!

After my meal, I rested a bit, and then my foster took me out to the dog run. Having closer fence rails, the dog run's enclosed area offered no means for escape. She removed my leash and went back into the house allowing much needed privacy for my dog run experience.

By this time, it was very dark outside with only a glimmer of light coming from a lamp in the sunroom. The shadows from the fence rails as well as the wind rustling through the bushes gave the dog run an eerie atmosphere that raised the hackles on my back. I had the entire area to myself, or so I thought. After I took care of my business, I started walking to the house and suddenly saw a figure hiding in the shadows that looked somewhat like a dog. Seeing that image startled me since I didn't notice the figure when I first came outside this afternoon. By this time, my hackles were crawling up and down my back as I crept quietly toward the figure. I wasn't sure what I would do when faced muzzle to muzzle with this stranger, but my curiosity was greater than my fear. Once again, I am not as smart as I think I am!

I boldly faced the shadowed figure and announced in my loudest bark that my name was Hector. By informing the figure that I was a big dog in a small body, I hoped that announcement made me sound very dangerous. Yet, nothing happened. The shadowed figure didn't move, and only the sound of the wind whistling through the bushes was heard. I then took a few more shaky steps and was face to face with the stranger. I was now ready to jump onto the "crazy train" in order to startle the intruder.

Imagine my surprise and embarrassment when I came face to face with the possible trespasser who turned out to be a weather-beaten, concrete statue of a dog in a sitting position. Since my imagination really got the best of me, I was glad Jake and Nigel weren't here to witness my courageous attempt to do battle with a concrete statue. Their howls of laughter would have echoed throughout the neighborhood.

When I went back into the house, my foster put the leash on my collar again, and we walked through the main room. On our way to the bedroom, we walked past the leather recliner, and I envisioned my strategic jump and vault onto the recliner's headrest. I just had to get furniture privileges in the very near future, but I knew I had to earn them.

Once in the bedroom, a spacious crate was positioned in one corner of the room. Inside the crate was a soft, welcoming cushion and some toys in case I got bored during the night. I enthusiastically jumped into the crate without any urging since I was really tired following the events of the past few days.

In addition to those activities, facing off for a battle with a concrete statue really took a lot out of this Short Stuff. While that earlier confrontation seemed quite silly, I really didn't know the shadowed figure was a statue when I challenged its presence in the dog run. In spite of the circumstances, my intent was to protect the property. In my mind, the actions were justified, and bravery prevailed!

As I curled up in the crate surrounded by the soft, fluffy cushion, my thoughts turned to seeing the leather recliner and imagining another recliner caper. Those thoughts held the promise of a good night's sleep, and I quickly drifted off to dreamland...

Another Escapade

Following a good night's sleep, I awakened to the sound of my foster filling my food bowl with kibble. The tinkling sound of the kibble bouncing into the metal food bowl elicited thoughts of the chicken and beans of yesterday's dinner. With each sound of the kibble dropping into the food bowl, I could almost taste the delicious morsels, and my appetite grew to new heights.

However, I was still in my crate waiting to be given my freedom to enjoy my breakfast. Then, I remembered that my foster was a bit of a jokester, so I needed to be prepared for any tricks she might throw at me. In this game of wits, I had some tricks up my front paws as well.

My foster came into the bedroom, said a very pleasant good morning to me and hoped that I had a good night's sleep. Since she was possibly a mind reader, she already knew that I had and was testing me. I wouldn't be fooled nor would I let my guard down with frivolous thoughts. Instead, I just focused my thinking about my good night's sleep and the breakfast awaiting me in the kitchen.

Then, she opened the crate and attached the leash to my collar once again. We traveled through the house to the dog run, and I was allowed freedom and privacy in that area. I said a pleasant hello to the concrete statue, did my business and walked back to the house. Just before I reached the door, I stopped to look at the statue. Since this figure might be the only friend I have while I am in this house, giving it a name seemed appropriate. I took a good look at it in order to find the perfect name. The statue looked quite weathered as though it had spent many, lonely years in this dog run and survived both the warmest and coldest weather. If it could talk, I'd bet it would have a story or two to share about dogs that have come and gone over the years. Maybe we both needed a friend. After thinking for a moment, I decided that Buddy was a good name for my new friend.

In the absence of my good friend Jake, I now had a voiceless confidant who listened to my woes without any judgment whatsoever. This new situation was great. I was temporarily placed in a nice home, getting delicious food, being treated well by a possible mind reader and now have a silent friend. I couldn't ask for more at this high point in my life. This foster placement was getting better and better each day!

My foster met me at the door and attached one end of a rather long, light leash to my collar and the other end of the leash to a loop on her jeans. She called this particular type of leash a tether which was meant to encourage bonding between us as well as keeping me in full view at all times. Where ever she went, I went. At first it was fine since I had a lot of room to play with some toys in the kitchen where she was finishing my breakfast preparation. But, when she decided to go to another room in the house, I had to follow whether I wanted to or not.

I struggled at first since I wanted to play with the ball from the toy box, but she kept on walking. I could either struggle or choose to follow her through the house. That tether was meant for more than just bonding since I was a captive on a long leash. However, I spotted the recliner and remembered my goal of furniture privileges and what I had to do to earn them. I quickly stopped tugging and joined in walking right beside her. I was ecstatic when she mentioned what a good dog I was. I hoped she was too busy to read my thoughts, or maybe she wasn't a mind reader after all. I'll have to think about that possibility later in the day.

Mealtime was finally here, and I was ready to play the mind-bending, food bowl game. I reversed my strategy of yesterday and instead of jumping and twirling around when I saw the food bowl in her hands, I just sat quietly on the floor in front of the food station. My foster just smiled, put the food bowl down in its place, said it was okay to eat and told me that I was a good dog. I have to give paw-points to her strategy. She was good at whatever game we were playing. I was extremely confused at that point but chose to just eat my meal that once again contained bits of chicken and some green beans. Delicious does not adequately describe my meal which actually seemed better than the one served last night. I decided that I liked this food game my foster and I were playing as long as meals like this were the rewards.

Following a rest period after my meal, my foster attached the smaller leash and told me that we were going on a neighborhood walk. I was excited about another new escapade because I really enjoy fresh air and exploration of new surroundings. As we left the house via the front door, I politely nodded to the statues that flanked the front door, walked down the driveway and onto the sidewalk. I momentarily stopped to look around the area that had so many new opportunities and was excited to begin the adventure.

We began our walk together, but then I decided that I needed to run ahead and explore on my own or at least to the extent of my leash. As I reached the end of the leash and tugged to go faster, my foster just stopped in her tracks. Now, the choking aspect of stopping suddenly didn't seem to bother her, but that quick stop certainly had quite the effect on me. I was caught between wanting my way and possibly choking or retreating in the form of a sitting position.

As soon as I sat on the sidewalk, the leash loosened and I was able to catch my breath. While I was self-resuscitating by sitting and breathing slowly, my foster just walked by me and didn't say a thing. To prevent being dragged by her brisk walk, I immediately caught up with her and walked by her side. She commented as to what a good dog I was and never even mentioned that I was almost choked by such a quick stop on her part earlier on the walk.

While I was thoroughly confused by all of her tactics, I resumed my running ahead when I thought it was safe to do so. She immediately stopped in her tracks. Once again, the taut leash attached to my collar brought me to a swift halt. As soon as I went into the sitting position, I was again able to breathe freely. If her strategy continues, I'm going to need to carry oxygen when out on walks. What was the purpose of this sequence of run ahead, get choked, stop pulling and then walk forward when the leash is loose? Some things just don't make sense to me!

I knew now that I was really dealing with a noteworthy adversary. When we stopped at the nearby park, I tried to figure out what was expected of me while on walks. If I pulled on the leash to get a faster glimpse of the area, she stopped walking. If I walked properly without pulling, we continued our walk in a pleasant and non-choking manner.

The answer hit me harder than a dog crate dropping on my head. As long as I don't pull on the leash, she won't stop walking, and I won't choke. What an interesting concept for dog walking. That strategy made a lot of sense and definitely saved wear and tear on my neck. Sometimes, I was not as smart as I thought I was. This neighborhood walk episode was certainly one of those moments. Nevertheless, I learned quickly, and the remainder of our walk was quite pleasant. My foster walked at a brisk pace, and I walked nicely within the length of my leash. All in all, I looked forward to our next walk in the neighborhood.

Later in the day, I spent some time in the dog run and, as foolish as it sounded, told Buddy all about my walking experience. While no comment came from my new friend as expected, I felt reassured talking about my day...even with a concrete statue. I really missed spending time with Jake and yes, even Nigel. After all, they were my very first friends, and they could communicate with me. For now, Buddy took their place and listened to my daily adventures. Sharing was definitely good for my soul. Right now, I was feeling very grateful for where I was and what was in store for me in the future.

Speaking of the future, I was told by my foster that tomorrow was a special day. I was going on a field trip to visit the animal hospital for my first, formal checkup. Another health procedure? How careful can this rescue group be in order to have heathy dogs available for adoption? I guess being a healthy dog is good for adoptions, but I just hoped more vaccinations weren't involved.

I was not going to think about that now. I had another great meal for dinner, but this time in addition to poached chicken, I had carrots! Yum! Of course, I sat quietly in order to get that food quickly, visited the dog run after my meal, said a quick good night to Buddy and then off to dreamland with thoughts of the leather recliner caper in my future…

Wellness Check

Today was the day for my wellness check at the animal hospital. All rescue dogs have to see a veterinarian to qualify for adoption. I can understand the intense scrutiny for safety purposes, but I'm just not sure what sort of examination awaited me. There have been so many changes in my life, and it seemed that every day had a new type of bodily inspection. Personally, I believed that I was a strong, hunk of canine masculinity, but would someone else feel the same? So many questions filled my mind as my foster prepared me for the field trip to the animal hospital.

I had been stalling for time by playing with a squeaky toy from the toy box when I heard her call out to me in a way that startled me. She urged me to hurry so as not to be late for the appointment and referred to me as Short Stuff! Short Stuff? How did she know my nickname? Now, I was certain that she was some sort of mind reader having magical powers. I really had to curb my free-wheeling thoughts when around her. If I could tell Jake and Nigel about my foster having such magical powers, that possibility would make their hackles go haywire! Truth be told, I was in for quite an adventure with this foster!

Without any change in expression, my foster readied me for the trip with no hint whatsoever that she knew my nickname. She reassured me that the exam was just a technicality, but nothing surprised me these days. We headed to the car, and I assumed my place in the crate that was situated in the back of the vehicle. From that vantage point, I was able to look out all of the car's windows. In spite of my anxiety regarding her familiarity with my nickname, I tried to relax for the ride to the animal hospital. I really had nothing to worry about with this examination. After all, I was quite healthy and nothing was wrong with me except for my vivid imagination. Even though I was filled with a bit of anxiety on a daily basis, that fact didn't make me less adoptable. I believed that my being somewhat anxious just made me vulnerable as well as lovable. Anyone looking for a forever pet would recognize those qualities and embrace them!

The trip to the animal hospital wasn't very long, and before I knew it, my foster had parked the car in the hospital's lot and was taking me out of the crate. Rather than put me down on the driveway, she held me close to her which tended to alert me to the possibilities of some surprises beyond that front door. What I knew for a fact was that as long as I was in her arms, I was safe. While she might be a mind reader and have some supernatural powers, I sensed that she truly cared for me and would let no harm come to me.

We entered the waiting room of the hospital where numerous dogs were waiting for their visit with the pet doctors called veterinarians. My foster registered me at the front counter, gave them my credentials as a rescue dog and took a seat at the back of the room while holding me close in her arms.

As I scanned the room, the dogs waiting for examinations were either howling, barking, whining, drooling or just sitting silently next to their owners. Just sitting in my foster's lap was a bit scary for me since I wasn't sure what I was supposed to do. Barking or howling didn't make any sense since I wasn't agitated, and whining only identified pain which was not my reason for being here. Forget about drooling since that behavior was so very unattractive as well as reminiscent of Nigel's tongue flop while sleeping. So, I looked to my foster for some direction. She just held me and told me that everything would be fine. Her reassurance was enough for me.

We waited for what seemed like a long time, but then I heard my name being called. Someone was actually calling my name, and hearing it gave me a sense of importance. My foster carried me into the examination room and placed me on a slippery, metal table. Within a short period of time, the veterinarian came in for my examination.

While I don't know what I anticipated, this doctor was beyond my expectations. In addition to her calm and reassuring voice, she had very kind eyes. I immediately felt that I could trust her and looked forward to my wellness check.

As she began her exam, she carefully listened to parts of my body with some sort of strange-looking instrument. Then, she examined the condition of my teeth, searched my rather large, upright ears for any sign of infection, looked deeply into my eyes and rotated my front and hind legs. As my strong legs moved exceedingly well during the leg rotations, I'm sure she was impressed with my compact, muscular structure. I believed that I was certainly ready and fit for adoption, and her diagnosis confirmed that fact. I gave one last look at her as we left and was actually grateful for this hospital visit. If all veterinarians conducted wellness checks like my doctor, what a wonderful world this would be!

With the examination concluded, my foster once again held me close to her heart as we went to the parking lot. She told me how happy she was that I was very healthy but was a bit sad because she knew someone would eventually adopt me. An adoption event was scheduled for this coming weekend. If I were adopted, I wouldn't live with her anymore. She would really miss me and the fun we had together. Believing that she was a mind reader, I hoped she read my thoughts and knew that I felt the same about her. Living with a mind reader wasn't so bad after all!

When we got back to the house, I was given a special treat. I no longer needed the tether because my foster said that she trusted me, and I now had the freedom to roam the house. I was so excited that I immediately ran to the leather recliner and just stared at it. I didn't dare jump on it because I had just earned her trust, but looking at it so closely gave me hope.

My foster sat comfortably on the couch to watch the television, and what happened next was beyond my expectations. She actually invited me to join her on the couch. Since I was a smaller dog, she told me that jumping onto the ottoman in front of the couch would make the jump easier for me. I didn't need a second invitation. Jumping from the carpet to the ottoman, up onto the couch and into my foster's lap was easy. Curling up with her and feeling so secure was an experience I had never imagined. Hoping that she read my mind, I wished that this moment would never end.

For a brief moment, I was embarrassed that my previous good behavior was based on wanting to earn furniture privileges. I did what was right for the wrong reasons, and that plan really backfired since my foster was just so kind to me. Now, I appreciated the value and the rewards of proper behavior. Jake would be very proud of me.

Thinking of the events that occurred today would certainly lead to a good night's sleep. Meeting the skilled veterinarian who concluded that I was healthy, saying goodbye to the tether since I earned my foster's trust, and finally being happily invited onto the furniture to curl up in my foster's lap was the icing on the dog bone. I was almost too excited to sleep, but remembering the events of the day gradually had a calming effect on me, and I gently glided into a deep sleep...

24

Wicker Chair Caper

Awakening in the morning following a restful sleep was invigorating. I was eager to greet the day as well as any new experiences that came my way. After all, since winning my foster's trust, having access to the entire house and furniture privileges, I just might be able to pull off the Leather Recliner Caper. If I were really lucky, I would then attempt the ascent to the headrest of the wicker chair in the sunroom. For now, I was just excited to face the day due to all of the possibilities for fun and enjoyment.

The next few days were busy and filled with new adventures. We went for well-behaved walks in the neighborhood, often visited playgrounds and shopped in areas that even had dog-friendly stores. Everywhere we went, people stopped and asked to pet me. I was a rock star in a dog's well-developed and masculine body! If I were able to write, I'd be signing paw-to-graphs on a daily basis! Don't even ask me about selfies!

Back at the house, I enjoyed the freedom to roam but preferred the company of my foster. I sat comfortably on her lap while she read or watched the television. She saw me jump onto the seat of the recliner, effortlessly vault onto the headrest and never shrieked or shouted about the possibility of my bouncing on the floor if I fell. She recognized my strengths and just let me live in my world as a dog having fun. Truth be told, I liked her more than ever for trusting me and allowing me to be myself.

One critical moment came the next day while we were relaxing in the sunroom. Soothing music was heard from the radio in the other room which just added to the somewhat lazy atmosphere of the day. Nevertheless, all was not entirely lazy for me because I periodically looked at that wicker chair facing the window with the intent of someday vaulting to the top of the headrest.

While I didn't know much about an adoption event, I did know that it held the possibility of my never returning to this house if I were chosen. My scaling the wicker chair had to be soon or not at all. With those thoughts in mind, I glanced at my foster who had been reading, looked at the wicker chair, threw caution to the wind, jumped onto the chair's cushion and curled up in a comfortable position. Since no reprimand was heard from my foster, I figured this first step toward scaling the wicker chair was a success.

My initial triumph with the jump to the wicker chair's seat cushion gave me the courage to attempt the total caper...jump from the floor to the seat cushion and finally, the vault to the headrest. Since I no longer needed to be crated and had freedom in the house when my foster left for errands, I waited until my foster went to the store for groceries to attempt this long-awaited caper.

I watched the car leave the driveway from the front window of the house and then raced back to the sunroom at full speed. Facing the front of the chair, I studied all of the angles in order to formulate the best approach for success. I decided to follow the same procedure as the successful one at Anne's house. I'd use speed to jump from the floor to the cushion and then reduce my speed for the vault. While extremely excited, I realized that this endeavor had no audience as the one at Anne's house and no carpet to cushion my fall should that unlikely event occur. Strangely, those facts didn't matter to me, and doing this was worth the risks. All that counted was a successful Wicker Chair Caper.

As my hackles tingled while I prepared for the jump, I suddenly thought this endeavor might not be the smartest move in case I fell off the headrest onto the hard, ceramic floor. The moment of caution quickly passed, and I prepared for the jump. Running at full speed, I jumped onto the wicker chair's cushion, twirled around to lessen my speed, and up I went to the top of the headrest. Because of the slower speed, my paws were able to grip the blanket that covered the edge of the headrest, and the Wicker Chair Caper was a total success!

Perched on the top of the headrest, I had an extended view of the entire yard through the nearby windows. I decided to stay at the top and watch the birds at their feeders with squirrels milling around the ground looking for buried nuts. I'm glad this escapade of mine was accomplished without an audience. Now, I considered the top of this wicker chair as my very special place where I could explore my private thoughts of the handsome man who saved me. Those thoughts filled my mind with hope that someday I might meet him again. Feeling that inner peacefulness of a successful endeavor and comforting thoughts of him, I was lulled to sleep right on the top of the headrest.

Since I was sleeping, I didn't hear my foster when she came home and didn't hear her enter the sunroom either. When she saw me perched on the top of the wicker chair's headrest, she quietly called my name so as not to startle me and cause a fall from my lofty perch. She commented on my acrobatic skills and hoped I had a good time planning that escapade. Now, I was really excited as well as convinced that she was a mind reader. Just wait until Jake and Nigel heard about all of my adventures with her as my foster...

25

Adoption Mania

My enthusiasm over the success of the awesome Wicker Chair Caper was short-lived with the knowledge that today we were going to something called an adoption event held at a suburban pet store. My foster explained to me that people interested in adopting would come to the store, look at the wonderful, available dogs and make life-changing decisions regarding adoption.

While I heard the words adoption event before, I wasn't aware of all of the technicalities. I learned that our personal photos and behaviors were highlighted on the organization's adoption website so interested people might be encouraged to complete adoption applications. I remembered my foster taking pictures of me, but I just thought she was making photographic memories of our foster time together. Perhaps she even captured my repeated Wicker Chair Caper for the web site, although that sort of escapade might not shine the best light on my favorable characteristics. In general, I'm glad that my behavior was mostly appropriate even though my original intentions regarding good manners were conducted for the wrong reasons.

Apparently, a great deal of information was gathered and checked before any adoption took place. However, the procedures didn't really take into account the dog's emotional aspect of leaving the foster's home. I believed that my foster and I truly bonded together during the time we shared. We followed routines, had expectations of each other and respected boundaries in terms of behaviors. I know that sounds silly coming from a dog who can't even speak the language, but experiencing sincere and loving care for the first time is such a great gift to a rescue dog.

I had just about given up on seeing the handsome man with the kind eyes who saved me. Any thoughts of his ever adopting me seemed vague since I probably wouldn't ever see him again. I knew that staying with a foster was a temporary placement, but possibly moving to some other home was simply too frightening for me. I was just getting used to this one and really feeling somewhat relaxed and happy. Nevertheless, as a rescue dog, I had no input into the situation and just had to go along with the plan. Not having any involvement in the situation, other than just being the dog, didn't seem quite fair. Of course, I still had a usable ticket on the "crazy train "if needed.

I wasn't in the best of spirits and dreaded going to the adoption event. My foster could tell by my body language that I wasn't up to my usual bragging rights in terms of being a big dog in the handsome, compact body of a small dog. In an attempt to cheer me up, she mentioned that Jake and Nigel would also be at the event. Hearing that I would see my friends again helped a lot since I had so much to talk about regarding adventures with my mind-reading foster, my concrete friend Buddy as well as my breathtaking Wicker Chair Caper. Maybe going to the adoption event wouldn't be so bad as long as I didn't get adopted by some stranger. I believed that the man with the kind eyes was the only one who could give me a forever home.

After my foster packed my bag containing treats, water and my very own folder of information, we headed to the adoption event. I was excited not just because this was a new adventure but also because I might see Jake and Nigel once again. As we pulled into a huge parking lot, I saw people walking in and out of the store with their pets. This event was definitely going to be fun!

I was carried into the store, and the sound of dogs barking was like music to my ears. Even though it was a bit noisy, I was with my own kind once again and immediately felt comfortable. In the middle of the store, volunteers were sitting at a long table...some with dogs and others just talking with people. At first, I saw one of the transport dogs with his foster and then, I saw my good buddies. There was handsome Jake, who looked even bigger than I remembered, standing politely next to his foster with no indication of any type of hibernation attempt. Next to Jake was Nigel who sniffed every child who passed by carrying an open bag of something edible. I'm sure he still hoped to find and taste corn chips. He looked rather dapper as long as he kept his tongue in his mouth.

My foster brought me over to my friends and put me down on the floor. I was so excited to see them that I jumped, danced and twirled around tangling my leash with theirs. At first it was a bit chaotic, but once the leashes were untangled, we sat nicely next to each other while our fosters chatted about their dogs.

I immediately told Jake and Nigel about my foster's mind-reading powers, her referral to me as Short Stuff, my making a silent friend who was actually a concrete statue as well as the successful completion of the Wicker Chair Caper. They were both amused by my antics and glad I had fun during my time with her.

Jake's good times with his foster included daily, long and invigorating walks in the neighborhood as well as in nearby parks. Watching the children playing on the swings and hearing their laughter gave him such a feeling of well-being. That comfort level was one that he only dreamt of having and reminded him of my belief in dreams coming true.

They also shared comfortable times relaxing while watching the television. His foster even allowed Jake to curl up on his couch which was such a treat and something Jake never thought possible due to his size. Jake said that fortunately his foster had a really large, comfortable couch! He had also perfected numerous, lengthy hibernation techniques at times during the day and attributed his success to the energy expended during his daily walks. Curled up on his foster's couch gave him his highest level of success! Jake hoped his foster might decide to adopt him since they had such fun together but understood that being with a foster was a temporary situation.

Nigel, on the other paw, had fun with his foster family consisting of a wife, husband and two children. Those children took dropping food on the floor to an art form, and Nigel was always ready and able to offer his clean-up services. He hadn't tasted a corn chip yet, but with the children eating all sorts of things during the day and dropping them all over the place, he remained hopeful for success some time soon.

After sharing our adventures, we settled down and watched the people who walked past the dogs waiting for that special someone to give them a forever home. A little while later, two very interesting dogs entered the store with their handlers, and each dog wore some sort of vest-like costume. The taller dog was a stunning, blonde Labrador Retriever named Brightie, and the other one was a handsome, white Jack Russell Terrier named Rufus.

While their handlers stopped to chat with our fosters, we learned that those two special dogs weren't wearing costumes at all but wore vests that designated them as representatives of their organization. They were actually therapy dogs who worked with children in hospitals and library programs. Jake, Nigel and I were amazed since we never imagined that dogs might have careers in the work force. Imagine a dog having a job! Maybe I could have a job someday helping children. I'd be proud to have that type of job. Needless to say, I'd look quite handsome in one of those vests!

After the two therapy dogs left the store with their handlers, we decided to just relax and enjoy the remainder of the event. Jake was sitting nicely and looking quite spiffy when a very tall man approached and seemed interested in him. Now, Jake was always such a confident dog. Yet, as the man approached, Jake snuggled tightly to his foster's leg, turning his head inward and giving the impression of being fearful. As soon as the man got nearer to him, Jake turned his head towards him, tilted his head a bit and gave that incredible smile that only Jake might give showing all of those bright, sharp teeth. That smile not only mimicked a menacing grimace but caused the man to back away quickly. Apparently, Jake was not going to be his forever pet!

Watching from the sidelines, I knew precisely what Jake had done. He deliberately sabotaged a potential adoption by giving his guard dog impression with just a friendly smile. I gave Jake a lot of credit for that gamble. While I never thought of Jake as being a gamer, today he was the top dog of games!

Nigel wasn't sure what happened since he was just concentrating on children walking past him. He figured that his chances of getting dropped edibles were greater with passing children. Surprisingly, Nigel was pretty smart in terms of this approach to his corn chip quest. However, not many people were passing by with children holding open bags of snacks.

Since the rescue organization had puppies at this particular event, the odds of people looking at us for adoption were slim. Puppies always received the undivided attention of both the young and old individuals looking for a forever pet. That fact baffled me since those of us who had been around the dog run a few times knew how to treat people, respected property and definitely weren't as needy as puppies. Older dogs just needed a bowl of water and a rubber bone with a treat inside. No fuss and no mess! That was the motto of dogs who have reached the age of reason!

Unfortunately, people just think puppies are cute, soft and cuddly. Just wait until the middle of the night when those "cuties" are howling and screeching to go outside in all sorts of weather. Cute, cuddly and soft only go so far in the human world when that happens on a daily basis. However, people need to find that out for themselves.

As time passed, people weren't coming to the pet store as steadily as they came in the morning hours.

My foster decided to leave a bit early and gathered my belongings in preparation to go. I said my goodbyes to Jake and Nigel in the hopes of seeing them again soon.

We left the pet store, and my foster settled me into my crate in the back of her car. As we started to leave the parking lot, I suddenly saw the handsome man with the kind eyes walking toward the entrance of the store. At first, I thought I was just imagining my seeing him, but he was wearing the same jacket that I remembered when he saved me. I still recalled the way the fleece lining of that jacket kept my wet and shaking body warm on that dreadful night. I couldn't believe that I was missing him again.

I wasn't sure what to do so I jumped back onto the "crazy train" once again. I howled, barked, twirled and bounced around the crate as I had never done before. My foster didn't know what was happening to me nor did she know how to make me stop. She drove the car into a parking space and spoke quietly in an effort to calm me from my frightful state. Once I realized that my efforts to gain the handsome man's attention were in vain, I just collapsed from the exhaustion of my behavior. How could I hold onto my hopes and dreams when fate just kept teasing me with sightings of this man?

I was devastated over missing that man again and spent time later that evening sharing my thoughts with Buddy. While I usually felt better after talking with Buddy, this evening's talk was not successful.

Once again, I questioned my beliefs in positive thinking, hopes and dreams. Going back into my foster's house, I perched my body on the top of the wicker chair's headrest, looked out the window at the darkened yard and engaged in a major pity party.

The next day, I adopted a better outlook on my life and decided that if I were destined to meet this man, that special encounter would happen. I just had to wait for fate to intervene, and my powers of positive thinking to give it a boost. Sharing those thoughts with Buddy in the morning felt so much better than last night's session.

The following week, my foster and I went to another adoption event. Jake and Nigel were there along with another group of adorable puppies. They were considered the flavored treats, and we were just the background props. Jake continued to use his smile as a deterrent to adoption by a stranger, and Nigel persevered in his quest for dropped edibles that might just be corn chips. Jake and I didn't have the heart to tell him that the odds were clearly against him.

The day was some sort of special occasion in that many children and dogs, who came into the pet store, wore costumes. The workers from the store gave the children candy, and the dogs wearing costumes were given special treats. We were amazed at the creativity of some of the outfits but really happy that our fosters didn't have us wearing some sort of get-up. Watching the costumed dogs casually walking by us was really quite interesting, and there was even going to be a contest for the most creative outfit in a little while.

As the contest time drew near, we could feel the excitement and mounting tension in the air. While the judges studied each of the contestants, the dogs and their handlers fidgeted due to the excitement. Finally, the judges made their decision. The winners were a Golden Retriever named Riggins and a black Labrador Retriever named Izzy. They were both dressed as crayons…yes, bright green and yellow crayons! Their costumes were amazing and obviously made by a creative and loving owner. The people in the store enthusiastically clapped their approval while dogs throughout the store barked and howled following the announcement.

I must say that the adoption events of the past two weeks had their highlights even though none of us were adopted. Last week, we met the therapy dogs named Brightie and Rufus. This week, we watched the costume contest where Riggins and Izzy won the prize for being dressed as crayons. We dubbed these past two weeks as Adoption Mania because of all the interesting things that took place.

One family was particularly interested in Nigel and hoped to see him again at the next adoption event. Introducing a dog to a family really took some thought, and hearing they were interested gave Nigel hope for a forever home. He just needed to keep his tongue inside his mouth in order to keep his regal status!

Jake consistently presented his signature smile to anyone interested in adopting him and took adoption sabotage to an art form with those brilliant, white teeth. I continued to watch the front door and scan the aisles in hopes of seeing the handsome man. The powers of positive thinking kept me hopeful that my dreams would come true. I just had to wait for that special dream to happen, and something deep inside reassured me that my time for a forever home would come...

CONCLUSION

During the weeks that followed, I spent my time in between adoption events, consulting with Buddy in the dog run regarding the affairs of the day, going for well-behaved walks in the neighborhood with my foster and looking out the window facing the yard from my perched position on the wicker chair. I spent a lot of time on that chair's headrest watching the antics of the birds at the feeders as well as devoting some time to well-deserved napping. Somehow, that perched position on the headrest of the wicker chair was just as comfortable as the soft pillow in my crate.

The adoption events went well and had numerous people coming to look at the dogs, but the puppies still had everyone's attention. Jake, Nigel and I just didn't know why people thought puppies were better forever pets than older dogs who might know their way to a person's heart minus the screeching and midnight outings. While it didn't make sense to us, we just watched the people cuddle and whisper sweet nothings to them. Surprisingly, they even allowed the pups to lick their faces. Don't people know where those puppies' tongues have been?

I still watched the front door and checked the aisles for the handsome man. In my mind, he was looking for me and would one day find me waiting just for him. Jake thought my wish might not ever come true and that I should keep myself open to other possibilities. Still, I was convinced the handsome man was definitely looking for me. Until that time, I always had a ticket to ride on the "crazy train" if anyone else were remotely interested in adopting me.

Nigel's quest for proving the pads of a dog's paws smelled like corn chips was ongoing. At the events, he positioned himself at the end of the aisle in order to catch any dropped morsel from a child's snack bag. He was determined to prove the corn chip theory, and nothing would get in his way of success.

Jake was convinced that his foster was going to adopt him. The bond between them grew during the past few weeks, and both Jake and his foster settled into a relaxed routine. Unlike his previous variations on hibernation attempts, Jake's current efforts were limited to the foster's couch. Apparently, Jake didn't have the need for awards and medals anymore. He finally found a sense of contentment with his foster that he had never known in his lifetime. Being chained to a fence so long ago was a faint memory for him. Now, he just waited until his foster made a decision about his adoption.

Jake continued his signature smile for anyone showing any interest in adopting him. That smile of his with those sharp teeth always made a person back away and reconsider him for their household. Jake had a clever side that I never expected, but I appreciated his ingenuity.

Before leaving for the adoption event this morning, I told Buddy that I had a good feeling about today and felt lucky about possible outcomes. If by chance I got adopted, I thanked him for listening to my conversations and for being a nonjudgmental friend. While he voiced no opinion, I was glad I mentioned my feelings. Today just might be my lucky day!

Proof of what happened next was enough to raise the hopes of my dreams coming true. When we reached the pet store, I noticed that there were no puppy pens in place for the little rascals. All the puppies had been adopted, and we were finally the featured act on the adoption program. Some dogs were barking, and others were just sitting peacefully next to their fosters. However, all of them were waiting for the right person to adopt them and offer a forever home.

Jake, Nigel and I assumed our regular positions at the event. Jake was clinging to his foster's side and scanning the area for would-be interested persons. He wanted to be prepared to offer his best smile if anyone approached. Nigel, on the other paw, was stalking children walking by with open snack bags hoping for dropped bits of treats. I maintained my station near the front door…watching, waiting and hoping for the handsome man to enter the store.

We were midway through the adoption event, when the family previously interested in Nigel returned to see him. The mother, father and son were happy to spend some time with Nigel. He was doing his best to appear regal in stature and was pulling out all of the biscuits in terms of maintaining his position as royalty as long as he kept his tongue in his mouth.

The young boy, carrying an open bag of snacks, was kneeling next to Nigel as his parents talked with his foster. Nigel could smell the contents of the bag and hoped to avoid drooling over the unfamiliar aroma wafting from the bag. Suddenly, a dog passing behind the boy barked at another dog. The powerful sound of the barking startled the boy and caused his snacks to fly all over the floor from the open bag. The mom immediately told the boy to pick up the corn chips because they might not be good for the dog.

Corn chips? Hearing those two words caused Nigel to quickly jump up from his position on the floor. Faster than a swarm of fleas jumping on a pack of dogs, he inhaled those morsels from the floor and left the floor spotless.

The incident happened so fast that Jake and I didn't realize what happened until it was over. We looked at Nigel who was curled up on the floor shifting his tongue containing bits of corn chips from one side of his muzzle to the other. While we wanted to look away in horror, Jake and I were mesmerized by the sight. The family looked almost as startled as we were.

Nigel, having swallowed all bits of corn chips, then proceeded to wrap his tongue around his nose. Most dogs can touch their noses with their tongues, but this sight was truly extreme and not at all a designation of royal behavior. Nigel then curled his paws slightly inward from his relaxed position on the floor, leaned down and sniffed the pads of his paws. Having done that pad-sniffing, Nigel gave out some outrageous, howling sounds that echoed through the pet store. Dogs all over the store began barking at the surprising sounds reverberating through the building. Nigel looked at us with the satisfaction of a job well done and exclaimed that the pads of his paws definitely smelled like corn chips! Following that declaration, he began to howl once again.

Jake and I had never seen Nigel so happy. Even though we often joked about his corn chip quest, he definitely worked long and hard for that discovery. The interested family thought he was so cute and decided to adopt him. While Nigel knew he was getting a forever home, he also figured he'd have access to corn chips and anything else the boy might drop on the floor. Life was good for him on all counts!

What a great adoption event this was turning out to be. A few interested individuals were looking for a large, stately dog and headed toward Jake. However, every time someone approached Jake, he resorted to his fake fear and large smile giving the appearance of a guard dog waiting for something to protect or eat. His foster recognized Jake's ploy weeks ago but wasn't sure if Jake wanted to stay with him as a forever dog. So, he took Jake aside, held him close and told him that he wanted to adopt him. While Jake certainly didn't understand all of his foster's words, he did recognize the gentle tone of his foster's voice. He just tilted his head and smiled one of his broadest smiles. Someone loved him for who he was in spite of his size and grimace-like smile. As his foster completed the adoption papers, Jake danced around happily and was finally going to his forever home!

Nigel and Jake said their goodbyes to me as they prepared to leave with their new families. I was truly happy for them even though I knew I'd probably never see them again. They were great friends at a time when I needed friendship the most. We shared so many Chez Shelter moments together when monotony, loneliness and despair might have filled our days. Nevertheless, their companionship changed the dark shadows to sunlight for each of us at a time when we needed help the most. Our friendship was permanently etched into a place in our hearts and would remain there forever. I still believed the handsome man would find me some day. I just had to be patient and continue to hope for my dreams to come true.

As I watched them leave through the front door with their families, both Jake and Nigel turned and gave me a farewell nod. I returned the nod and settled down with my foster and a few of the rescue dogs who remained at the event. Since the event was almost over, we were sitting off to the side and out of the view of people entering and exiting the store. I wasn't paying any attention to the front door or the aisles since we were going to leave soon. Instead, I decided to take a quick nap before heading back to the house. I closed my eyes, thought about all of the wonderful events that occurred today and was on my way to a restful snooze.

While drifting in and out of my attempt at dozing, I thought I heard a vague yet somewhat familiar, human voice. Initially, I thought my dreams had now taken on a vocal quality, but the voice actually sounded real. I woke up but still had my eyes closed when I heard the voice again. Only this time, the man was asking for specific information about a small, black Chihuahua. He explained how he had found this dog abandoned in the rain months ago and took him to a shelter for safety. While he really wanted to adopt the dog, he was going out of town for a few weeks and wouldn't have a good place for him until he returned. Visiting the shelter upon his return, he was told that the dog had been one of a few dogs chosen by a rescue group for future adoption.

He told the volunteer that something about that little dog shivering in the rain immediately gripped his heart. He felt an unfamiliar, loving connection to the dog and was determined to find him. He looked for the dog for quite some time but never found him at any events. The volunteer told him that they only had one dog named Hector who fit that description.

Upon hearing my name as well as the sound of the man's voice, I immediately jumped up from my napping position and tried to match the voice with a face. When I looked, the handsome man with the kind eyes was standing just a few feet away from me. I was stunned and tried blinking my eyes numerous times in case I was hallucinating.

When the man saw me, he did something totally unexpected. Most people interested in dogs at the events came up to them, stroked their heads and talked to them. This man didn't do any of those behaviors at all. Instead, he sat down on the floor and waited to see if I would come to him. This kind man was giving me the choice of choosing him for my forever family.

Without any hesitation, I ran as fast as I could and jumped into his lap. This kind and gentle man would never know how much I dreamt of this moment over the past few months. All of my hopes and dreams of a forever home with him were coming true. I'd pinch myself, but why risk defacing such a compact and magnificent physique?

While curled up in his lap as he gently stroked my head and rubbed my paws, I thought of all the events of the past few months that led to this particular day. Being rescued by him in the rain and his bringing me to the shelter was just the beginning of a journey that tested my beliefs in dreams and a life worth living.

Meeting Jake and Nigel helped me endure the most difficult moments at Chez Shelter. The strong bond of friendship we shared helped each of us through the sad times. Surviving the time at Chez Shelter together and finally leaving was definitely bittersweet due to the apprehension of going to Who-Knows-Where with perfect strangers. What were we thinking, or were we thinking at all?

Recalling the boredom of the transport was only interrupted by the ghastly trip to the Rest Stop. Thanks to Jake's large paws and the path he planned for us, we made it safely past that problem. Jake's courage will long be remembered for the sacrifice he made for us that day.

Learning acrobatic skills from Dino and Angel as well as being guided by the leadership of gentle Gus helped us in our transitions to foster situations. Jasper, the cat, was inspirational in terms of his courage, his sense of humor and his message to me regarding disrespect toward others. Each of those dogs and that wise cat had an impact on my life.

While feeling so secure in the handsome man's lap, I felt a bit disloyal to my foster. In spite of my earlier belligerence, she offered kindness, gave me a safe place to stay, cared for me in such a special way and allowed me to be myself. Under her supervision, I learned eating and walking etiquette, cuddled with her on the couch while watching television and repeatedly spent time looking at the antics of the squirrels and birds in the yard from my wicker chair perch.

In so many ways, my foster prepared me for this moment in time. Knowing I had been shuffled from place to place, she took me in to her home and gave me a safe place to stay. With tolerance, patience and love, she prepared me for the next chapter in my life. My heart definitely had room for her and the memory of her kindness.

As the handsome man completed all of the paperwork for my adoption, I looked around the room and imagined Jake and Nigel giving me their nod of approval. A new chapter was beginning for them as well as for me.

While doubts sometimes filled my mind about my future, I relied on positive thinking to get me through those challenges. I remained steadfast in my belief that someday someone would see me and be totally captivated by my charming personality, good looks and distinctive, muscular physique! What was not to like?

Finding a forever home has been my hope for as long as I can remember. Dreams of that wish coming true governed my actions in many ways. Sometimes, being a dreamer isn't the most popular way of life in the canine pack, but being true to myself and always relying on hope for the future is a way of life for me.

My adoption was finalized, and I was ready to begin the new chapter in my life. As my foster handed my leash to the handsome man, she hugged me and wished me well. I'm glad I said goodbye to Buddy this morning just in case my feeling of this day being my lucky day was real. I'll surely miss our conversations.

In my short life, I experienced abandonment, hunger, loneliness and fear. I also met some wonderful dogs and a wise cat along this journey. They helped me through moments of despair as well as taught me how to survive in my search for a better life. What sustained me through the difficult times was my unwavering belief that I not only deserved a better life, but that special life was waiting for me just around the corner.

I have lived my life trusting in the strength of being hopeful as well as being a steadfast dreamer. Today, walking into a new life and a forever home with someone who loves me proves that dreams really do come true.

Thank you for sharing my journey...

Hector

Cast of Characters

Hector

Jake

Nigel

Dino

Angel

Jasper

Gus

Ann

Cast of Characters Continued...

Kessen

Buddy

Riggins and Izzy

Rufus

Brightie

Handsome Man

The Author

Jennifer Rae Trojan, who writes as Jennifer Rae, lives in a suburb of Chicago, Illinois. As a retired high school guidance counselor, she and her husband worked with various assistance dog organizations as puppy raisers, puppy sitters and volunteers with animal assisted therapy. In addition to those activities, Jennifer and her husband gave presentations at libraries, in schools and to several community groups regarding the journey of the assistance dog and how these events related to her books.

Following the loss of her husband, Jennifer embarked on a new chapter of her life. Joined by her friend, Pam Osbourne, they developed a power point presentation combining the roles of both the assistance dog and the therapy dog. Together, they shared their combined information with community organizations.

Jennifer's involvement as a volunteer with A.R.F. (Animal Rescue Foundation) led to the writing of her current book...*Hector's Hope*. According to Jennifer, sharing Hector's journey from his point of view beginning with his abandonment to a loving, forever home was not just a creative endeavor but a true labor of love.

Acknowledgements

The unfortunate journey of abandoned and forgotten dogs and cats is one of hunger, loneliness, sadness and survival. Through the efforts of dedicated volunteers affiliated with rescue groups, numerous dogs and cats are saved from the streets and shelters in an effort to assist in finding forever homes for them.

While I thank those individuals, who helped in having Hector's story come alive, there are certain individuals who deserve special recognition for their efforts in getting his story onto the printed page.

 First, I must sincerely thank my dear husband **Chuck Trojan** for his past support and encouragement. Even though **Chuck** is no longer with me, his gentle voice is ever-present and guides me every step of the way while creating a story.

Kim Stephenson, of PawPrintsPix Photography, was responsible for creating the unique cover templates, assisting with the back cover  collage as well as enhancing each of the photos used in the book. **Kim** worked toward and earned the status of Master Photographer (M.Photog.) in her field. Her skill and expertise are evident in terms of the quality of her images and cover designs. **Kim's** talents, patience and generosity are greatly appreciated.

Pam Osbourne served as an exceptional consultant, proof reader and designer of the collage of dogs and cats for the back cover. Her expertise was vital to the final printing process and contributed significantly to the completion of the book. **Pam** is also a good friend as well as a gifted writer.

Kathleen Deist, the Goddess of Grammar and Punctuation, served as one of the proof readers for this book. As a former English teacher, her expertise in the areas of grammar and punctuation proved extremely helpful toward its completion. Please don't hold her accountable for my not using  semicolons. She indicated their usage in some paragraphs, but I disregarded them and clarified my position in the disclaimer. Having **Kathleen** as a consultant for my books has been an incredible experience; having her as my friend is the greater gift.

 **Carol DeMaio**, the Comma Queen and a valued friend of many years, served as one of my proof readers. As a former teacher, her creative insights as well as her attention to detail provided invaluable assistance. **Carol** never once allowed our friendship to stand in the way of constructive criticism. I truly appreciated her honesty, time, expertise and above all, her enduring friendship.

Special thanks to the volunteers of **A.R.F. (Animal Rescue Foundation)** for their heartfelt and tireless efforts to rescue animals in dire  A.R.F. - Animal Rescue Foundation situations. They actively strive toward finding forever homes for those animals through a vigilant adoption process. Knowing the animals are going to loving homes is a gift to all involved.

I'd also like to thank A.R.F. for granting permission to use their logo in the Dedication and Acknowledgements of this book.

Thank you to all the **Special People** who choose to adopt a pet and to the **Rescue Groups** around the country for the tremendous job you do for forgotten and abandoned animals. You are their hope for a life in a loving, forever home.

IN MEMORIAM

Baily, Bandit, Bear, Brightie, Britches, Buddy, Echo,

Etienne, Finn, Gus, Jingles, Jody, Kelyn, Kessen,

King, Linus, Magnum, Navarre, Phoebe, Tico,

Pookie, Roscoe, Rudy, Rufus, Sammy, Shamus,

Turin, Vanessa, Vartan, Wynston, Zachary, Zoe

**They gave us unconditional love
and
left paw prints on our hearts.**

CPSIA information can be obtained
at www.ICGtesting.com
Printed in the USA
BVHW092029221021
619639BV00001B/1